PRAISE FOR *DOG*

"Yishay Ron's gripping, haunting *Dog* performs the magic act that all novelists seek but rarely achieve: to lure readers inside worlds they have neither lived nor can ever imagine—and yet, somehow, know that they have arrived. This is a postwar novel par excellence, with its lingering torments and redemptions of the aftermath."
—**Thane Rosenbaum**, author of *The Golems of Gotham, Second Hand Smoke,* and *Elijah Visible*

"In the tradition of the best war novels, Yishai Ron's *Dog* reminds us of our confounding inability to learn from the past. With pity, rage, compassion, and despair, Ron shows the dreadful toll war takes on man and beast. The novel also provides an unsentimental and humane depiction of contemporary Israel, a country many people believe they know. In the end, and often with gallows humor, *Dog* affirms the fragility and validity of life."
—**David Bezmozgis**, author of *The Betrayers*

"*Dog* reads like a cry that rolls forward at an incredible pace, carried by the flow of the plot. At times, there's a desire to pause, to grasp onto something at the edges, but—just like the characters in the book—you can't. The characters are tough. Life has struck them hard, and they are laid bare, yet they are portrayed with a compassionate gaze, with empathy and honesty."
—**Yishai Sarid**, author of *The Third Temple, Victorious,* and *The Memory Monster*

"This is a remarkable book—powerful in its ability to open the world of PTSD to the reader. It reveals the partial destruction, the entanglement with a different kind of reality, the destructive paths of escape, and the surprising openings toward hope."
—**Asa Kasher**, Professor Emeritus, Tel Aviv University, Lead Author of the IDF Code of Ethics

"*Dog* took me by storm and struck a deep, emotional chord in me. It is a powerful story on so many personal, social, and political levels, and I realized that I must turn it into a movie."
    —**Eran Riklis**, Director & Producer, *The Syrian Bride, Lemon Tree, Reading Lolita in Tehran*

"Terrible and wonderful, heartbreaking and heartfelt—if literature has any hope of making us better people, it will be through the brutal, beautiful honesty of works like Ishi Ron's remarkable *Dog*."
    —**Shalom Auslander**, author of *Hope: A Tragedy* and *Feh: A Memoir*

"A profound, original, thought-provoking novel. To read it is to have your heart broken."
    —**Noa Yedlin**, author of *Stockholm*

"A formidable, painful novel. Rare emotional intensity."
    —**Zeruya Shalev**, author of *Pain: A Novel*

"Ishi Ron's unsettling novel, *Dog*, serves up a chilling account of despair, redemption, and murder in the aftermath of war. Returning from Gaza to Tel Aviv, a decorated Israeli officer who has assumed the name 'Geller' drowns his trauma in heroin as he navigates a new life among misfit junkies. Enter Dog, the novel's eponymous mongrel, who offers a deeply perceptive, highly canine perspective on Geller's suffering. Both convincing and disquieting, Ron adds his powerful voice to a rising generation of veteran novelists who capture the psychological pain and dislocation of modern warfare."
    —**Jacob M. Appel**, author of *Einstein's Beach House*

"Dog should come with its own Surgeon General warning: This highly suspenseful and unexpectedly lyrical book could be hazardous to your health. Read at your own risk!"
    —**Roya Hakakian**, author of *A Beginner's Guide to America for the Immigrant and the Curious*

DOG

DOG

Yishay Ishi Ron

—————

Translated from the Hebrew by

YARDENNE GREENSPAN

SONCATA PRESS
NEW YORK, NEW YORK

This edition first published in 2025 by Soncata Press LLC.
With offices at:
340 W 57th Street, Suite C
New York, NY 10019
www.soncatapress.com

Hardback ISBN: 979-8-9926452-3-1
Paperback ISBN: 979-8-9926452-4-8
E-book ISBN: 979-8-9926452-7-9
Audiobook ISBN: 979-8-9926452-6-2

Library of Congress Control Number: 2025933651

Cover design by Howard Grossman
Author Photo by Yael Orvachon, 2025

Dedicated to the combatants

whose eyes have seen things

that their minds refuse to forget

CHAPTER ONE

A few devious rays penetrate the cracks between rot-festering slats that someone nailed years ago to the spot where shutters should be. They slice through cold, bitter, almost toxic air and accentuate the tiny specks of dust that mingle with pigeon droppings in hidden corners.

At first, the twinkling light appears capable of driving out the darkness, but the rays only reveal broken walls and peeling paint, underneath which mold laps like a devouring monster at decomposing frames that had once housed handsome doors. Red, orange, and grass-colored floral patterns lie faintly visible underneath the grime of the floor tiles. The tiles must have been purchased in the beginning of the previous century in the Wieland factory, not far from the Ottoman train station that is now a hip, historically preserved shopping center. The walls tower almost fifteen feet high, and from the ceiling pokes the base of an elegant chandelier, of which not even a shadow remains.

The stench pummels one's nose like a rock. For years, homeless people have been dropping in and out of this place, leaving only their excrement behind. The remnants of a bonfire someone lit in the middle of the room, perhaps last winter, are smudged along the ground like a black, smoky tattoo.

This morning, a heavy rain infiltrated the broken roof tiles, pooling the debris all around me into puddles streaming narrowly along the floor, until one of the murky creeks found its way into my sleeping bag and woke me up before the desire for heroin could do the same.

I used to be as strong as basalt. Most of the time I was content, too foolish to recognize my own sadness. In spite of the drugs that addle my brain, I remember the moment everything broke in great detail: the fragrance of Tel Aviv at nighttime, black and sweet, the burning flavor of whiskey. It was neither hot nor cold that night, and the air seemed to penetrate right through my skin and flesh and bones. I was nothing but a ghost. Above me hovered a festive moon, and all around it, like a mobile hanging over a bassinet, were the stars. That celestial display could have served as a fantastic backdrop for almost any powerful moment in life. The night was perfect, apart from the ways in which it reminded me of Gaza.

That night, a bomb went off in my head—though it was too small to fit all those killed, on our side and theirs, with the metallic smell of blood rising from the scorched flesh and camouflaged faces of fighters, from machine guns and two-way radios. There were no stretchers or uniforms or commands, no rations or smelly canteens or roll call. There was only fear, footsteps, and a dead dog inextricably linked together.

Earlier that week, Brazil won the 2013 Confederations Cup, and two days later General Abdel Fattah el-Sisi overthrew Egyptian President Morsi in a military coup. I also remember a team hangout in Boaz's yard. We were a very unified group back then. Even Avihai, the unit commander, showed up because of everything that had happened in Gaza over the previous winter, when we lost Yehoram, and Boaz was hit by shrapnel, and I took two bullets. Avihai came directly from counterterrorism training and squeezed our arms one by one like an emotional dad. But after that he just sat there with his tough face, his uniform and ranks, his boots and rifle, and watched with a critical smirk as the rest of us drank our asses off and messed around, maybe even acting out on purpose, because we were known as the wild bunch.

Doron balanced Smirnoff bottles on his head to everyone's applause, then began to dance to an imaginary beat, and we all kept our eyes on the bottles, expecting them to crash to the ground at any moment. I felt the bizarre sensation that I too was poised in that place between steadiness and shattering. The guys danced, and Boaz's mother circled the room with food and drinks, because as far as she was concerned, everything to do with her son was pure and unadulterated, and she was proud of all of us for fighting in an elite unit. She respected us.

I'd returned from Japan two months earlier, and even though I'd broken up with Zohar, I felt it was a rather tranquil, pleasant time. I was an honorably discharged officer soon to enroll in law school, and Avihai was talking to me about doing reserve duty two months down the line. It was all good.

I kissed and hugged my friends goodbye. It was a little past midnight and I'd already had two cups of Turkish coffee and felt sober enough to get on my motorcycle. I drove from Herzliya to Tel Aviv and parked outside my building. I decided it wasn't too late for another drink, and if I was lucky perhaps I'd meet someone interested in getting a closer look at the scars left by two bullets I'd taken during the previous year's Operation Pillar of Defense. So I headed to my regular bar, wearing a black leather jacket, jeans, a white T-shirt, and the sneakers Zohar had bought me in Japan. The gun I carried for work was in the holster against my hip. I took a right on Amsterdam Street and kept moving toward Immanuel the Roman Street. I heard footsteps behind me, beating down the sidewalk like a division of soldiers, a kind of metallic rumbling, military boots marching, ready for battle. All at once, there were tens of thousands of footsteps just like those. A fear bomb exploded inside of my body. Reality vanished, and there was no more Tel Aviv, no buildings or streets or illuminated windows, no yards or fences or cars. I reached for my hip and took hold of the gun's cold grip, a gesture as automatic as blinking, an instinct rather than anything learned. I pulled out the gun, cocked it hard against my belt, pointing it downward, and turned around in a flash. I grabbed him by the throat, pushed him against the wall, and held the gun to his chest.

I didn't notice he was just a teenager, about seventeen years old. I didn't notice he was dressed up for a night out, gel in his hair, pierced ears and upper lip. I didn't hear him calling for help. All I saw was the dog Yuval had shot in the head when we were in Shejaiya. Footsteps, fear, dead dog.

Then I smelled his cologne. Eternity by Calvin Klein washed over me, and suddenly the fabric of his shirt was thin and flimsy and his eyes were filled with terror and his mouth pursed with shock. And there was urine, too. I was standing in a puddle pooling on the sidewalk after streaming down the front of his pants. His fear and my fear comingled until I could no longer tell mine from his. I pinned him against the wall, then let go of him as he collapsed into his own bodily fluids, whimpering in his wretchedness, suddenly appearing more delicate and fragile then an eggshell. I unloaded the Glock, caught the bullet as it popped out, and returned it into the magazine, slipping the gun into its holster wordlessly. I left him on the sidewalk and hurried away.

I sat down on a bench on the avenue and wanted to cry, but there were no tears, only fear, pain, and confusion. The fear still tickled the edges of my body like a flame consuming paper. The dog from Shejaiya fluttered through my head, the moment when he took the bullet and collapsed to the ground. For a second, there was no sign of anything, no blood, and then all at once he began to writhe and twitch, and blood flowed under his head, forming an enormous red puddle.

A girl rode past on her bicycle, a couple strolled hand in hand, a woman walked two poodles, cars rolled slowly from one red light to the next. The city was beating at its regular life pace, but I felt untethered, as if watching myself from the outside, sitting on that bench, heart racing, electric currents jolting my extremities, intense nausea gripping my abdomen. A heavy weight settled inside my chest, making it hard to breathe. I searched for my cigarettes. A few minutes went by before I recalled I'd quit smoking. I sat there, sweating and trembling, sensing imminent disaster. I buried my face in both hands, and without even realizing it, let out a wail. I pictured that kid peeing himself, convinced he was about to die.

I got up and started running. Tel Aviv became anywhere—Tokyo, Paris, Shejaiya. I didn't look around, letting my sneakers carry my legs where they might. I ran because fear wasn't as fast as my feet. Panting consoled me and the effort soothed me. When I stopped and bent down, leaning my hands on my knees to settle my breath, I realized I was outside of my building.

Tired and drained, I locked the door behind me and turned the place upside down in search of a cigarette, but it was a no-go. In the bathroom, I peeled off my clothes as if they were infected with madness, then examined myself in the full length mirror Zohar had left behind. My muscles were swollen, the flying tiger tattoo—the commando symbol that our entire team had gotten—stood out on my chest. The other teams had pins on their uniforms, but we had the tiger right under our skin. Now it frightened me. The narrow eyes, the sharp teeth, the claws breaking out of its large paws. It seemed to be pouncing at me from right out of my own chest. I couldn't bear to look at it. The taste of blood spread over my tongue—metallic, salty, dizzying. It felt as if the winged beast was slicing through my heart. I rubbed my thumb against the ink, trying to erase it, but it just kept staring at me mockingly. Then I grabbed a razor and ran the blade down the tattoo, making a deep cut, then another. Blood began to run down my body in thin downward streams. I looked at my face in the mirror. It was covered with stubble that was only a little shorter than the cropped hair on my head. My cheekbones were prominent, my lips full, and above them was that familiar tunnel leading to the bottom of my nose. But my eyes were filled with madness. I ran a hand down my cheek and pulled on the flesh as if kneading dough. I was no longer myself.

I turned on the water in the shower, letting it pour down on me and wash off the red tracks that continued to emerge from between the thin lips I'd sliced through my chest, the tiger's tears. I leaned against the wall and allowed myself to slide down until I was sitting on the shower floor. For the first time since childhood, I cried loud bellowing wails from the bottom of my navel. I cried and cried and didn't know why.

———

I wake up the next morning, curled up in a corner in a muddy, putrid quagmire. I have three gram-bags so the whole world can go up in flames as far as I'm concerned. I just want to shoot up before Crutchy Zvi or the Georgian show up. I pull out one of the baggies from an inside pocket I've sewn into the lining of my jacket, a little cache to prevent anyone from robbing me while I'm asleep or unconscious. I pull out a small LED flashlight and point it around me to find the can. An empty can is safer than a spoon, especially when you've got shaky hands. The Georgian taught me this trick: you slice a large door into a soda can, turn it upside-down, and place the junk in the small dimple at the bottom of the can. Then you slip a lighter inside and warm the stuff from below, like a little lantern. My hand searches for a syringe in the pocket of my cargo pants, and I pull out a 10/3 mL with a short, thin needle. I start to feel a lot better, as if I've already injected. I wrap a military tourniquet around my left arm, pull the strap hard to tighten it, then mix powder with a bit of water in the empty can, light a small fire underneath it, then move it in tight circles to warm everything up equally. I don't want the liquid bubbling, just warm enough for the powder to dissolve. If it boils, some of the junk will be lost. I dip a small filter into the solution and tuck the edge of the needle in, drawing only the clean and filtered stuff, slowly filling the syringe, tapping my finger against it to separate the air from the liquid, feeling like a doctor preparing a life-saving treatment. While the heroin cools down inside the syringe, I run a finger over my arm, searching for the bump of a vein. I can find a spot with my eyes closed, from back in the days when the battalion sent me to medic training. A ray of sun filters through the slats blocking the window and strips my arm of darkness. I grab an alcohol wipe and clean the blue ridge of the vein carefully. Each and every cell in my body cheers as I insert the needle, pull out a bit of blood, inject a bit of junk, pull out blood again and inject junk again, then push it all the way into my blood stream, which drives the heroin into my heart at a speed of half a meter per second. Euphoria glues together the shards of my soul. I sit down on the armchair facing the slatted window, close my eyes, and dive into a sea of calm that knows no sorrow, depression, or anxiety. Specks of dust float inside the sunbeams like tiny creatures revealed under the lens of a microscope. I can sense the morphine molecules attaching to opioid receptors inside my brain, filling me with a calmness that camouflages as happiness.

I light a cigarette and smoke it with a dry mouth. In a few minutes, I'll go down to Ovad's café for a cup of coffee, but first I pull my phone from my pocket. I haven't used it as a phone for a long time, but I always keep it charged so I can watch that old Uri Geller video. I turn on the phone and go into the YouTube app. A blue light glows in the dark. The video was taken in the 1970s and it's as scratched and jumpy as if it had spent years lying in a World War II archive. I follow the clip like a student watching an instructional video. Five minutes later I turn off the phone and remove the chain with the silver spoon from around my neck. Whenever cops stop me, they assume I use it to cook up. Idiots. Anyone can see the spoon is clean, shiny, and perfect. A flame has never touched it. I don't use it for shooting up or for eating. It's my Uri Geller spoon. I hold it in my left hand, rubbing it with concentration, carefully running a finger over it, applying no force, and praying with all my heart for it to bend, just like in that video.

What I do with the spoon is not a ceremony, it's training. I lose myself in meditation, in deep, slow breathing, trying to fill my lungs with air clean of the disruptions of the outside world. All my energy is focused on the spoon. My thoughts surround it, and I beg it to bend for me, just once will do. *Please, bend, please,* I plead. A ray of light catches it and shoots right into my eyes, like the magical twinkle of a fairy. I think about nothing, closing my eyes and imagining that one day it'll work, and my life will transform. When I can bend Uri Geller's spoon, I'll be God.

CHAPTER TWO

Dog was nameless and homeless before Zukerman adopted him. Before that, there is not very much he can recall with clarity, but sights and smells from the past often float into his consciousness. A stubborn fight in the cruel competition for a nourishing nipple, scuffling and playing with his brothers and sisters, his mother's rough tongue against his coat. His brothers were handed out unceremoniously to the neighborhood children, and his fate was no different. He was placed in a cardboard box and given to a boy, even had the privilege of sleeping under the same roof as his new family for several days, before the father decided that a stupid puppy incapable of being housetrained ought to find a different home.

He was handed off to another, more patient family, who took him on walks three times a day, where he enjoyed the onslaught of exciting aromas, marked every corner and pole with determined peeing, and shat in his regular spot every day. It was a loving family whose odors were etched in the dog's memory for the rest of his life. The mother was a large woman with kneading caresses and a comforting, velvety voice. The father would return home every evening and pat Dog with his large, heavy hands as Dog jumped up to lick his face. He always smelled of tobacco mixed with sweet cologne. There was also a baby, who spent most of his time in a crib, and whose crying summoned the members of the household at all hours of the day and night. There was a little boy, energetic and wild and unique in his love. He and Dog would run around, rolling on the floor and losing themselves in cuddles and kisses and belly rubs. It seemed to Dog that the long days of summer would never come to an end.

He remembers the tumult and enthusiasm in the household as everyone pulled suitcases and duffel bags from closets and joyously filled them with clothes and possessions, as happy as if they were looking forward to a fragrant, filling meal. He frolicked right along with them with tail wagging and ankle sniffing and skipping.

Then the father helped him into the car, and they drove for a while before arriving at an unfamiliar place, without dirt, where all the smells were foreign. They got out of the car, and the father rubbed his head and got back into the car by himself, leaving Dog all alone. He watched the car moving away, then sat down and waited to be picked up and returned home. Even when everyone left, Dog knew they always came back. So he waited a long time, then walked around for a bit, and sat back down. But nobody showed up. His family didn't come back for him, and he remained on his own, scared and sad.

There were other events that had left their mark on him: the cat that savagely attacked him in defense of her kittens, scratching his sensitive nose. The fleas that attacked him in the derelict public bomb shelter, stinging him mercilessly. The man who called him over, waving a delicious smelling hot dog at him, then delivering a swift kick in the stomach instead.

Eventually, he was caught and taken to a pound, where anxiety took over him, leaving him restless. He lay in a small metal cage, fearing the other dogs, as well as the people who cleaned the cages with sweeping brooms and scrubbing brushes and slamming doors. He watched figures moving past him, heard yelling and barking, and smelled constant confusing aromas.

If it weren't for Zukerman's patience, the petting that continued into the night, the nice shower they took together, the devoted care, and the co-sleeping in his soft bed, he would never have trusted humans again. Zukerman was a special human being. When he came to the pound, he wandered among the cages, and something made him pause and look at Dog. He was wearing an ironed suit and a blue striped necktie, but he still crouched down like a child and reached a long arm through the bars.

Now Dog licked the wound on his leg to try and alleviate the pain. The bleeding had stopped two days earlier, but his leg pounded with awful pain. That morning, he'd lapped some water from a bucket outside a building, and the previous day a boy had tossed over some leftover sandwich. He waited for the kid to leave, then ate with slow hesitation.

The pain upset him more than the hunger. His tongue felt the tattered fur and the torn skin, but he was dealing with the pain. It hurt as if a car had run him over. But it wasn't a car, it was a big dog. He didn't stand a chance. Had he not made it out in time, the affair would have ended with far worse than bruises and one deep leg wound.

One day, Zukerman didn't wake up. He lay in bed and Dog knew there was no more life inside him. He sat beside him for three days, licking his face in an attempt to wake him, though he knew the man was no different than the bird carcasses he'd witnessed on their long walks. Dog was hungry, but he wouldn't leave Zukerman's side apart from a few quick jaunts to drink from the toilet bowl and relieve himself in the hallway. Then there was a knock at the door, and Dog barked but Zukerman couldn't open it, so whoever it was left. After a while they came back, opened the door, and found Zukerman in bed. Then more people showed up and there was chaos. They took Zukerman away and wanted to take Dog too, but he barked as loud as he could and wriggled out between their legs out to the stairwell, then into town.

He ran fast down the route he always took with Zukerman, passing by all the familiar smells, not stopping to pee until he was far away from his home. Since then, he'd been wandering the city on his own. He waited in a narrow alley for the rain to stop, then came out limping. He had to find something to eat. Water pooled in large puddles on the road and sidewalks, and a cold wind blew between the buildings. He smelled many dogs, stronger than him, then cats, food, and people. He smelled thousands of odors, recognizing only a few. Then he saw the dump. The morning was long gone by the time he entered the damp dimness and a swell of curious smells. He found some scraps of food and ate them, then lay down among soft fabrics, a roof over his head and walls to protect him from the wind.

CHAPTER THREE

After Ovad made me coffee, I went to beg for change. Our agreement is, he makes me a latte in a disposable cup, and I don't bother his customers. The beverage warms up my hands and esophagus, and the heroin does the same thing for my heart. I've been taking heroin for less than a year, but I've already become addicted and developed a tolerance more characteristic of a years-long user. Like all users, I remember the first time I shot up. A hit of heroin releases a thousand times more dopamine than an orgasm. If you inject the right dose and the right kind of stuff, it's like making love with God. I lay down on the bed, euphoric, not believing what I was feeling. My body was so relaxed I thought I was floating on air; a million lips kissed my skin and soul, and nothing bothered me.

My father was a vegetable by that point, connected to his drip irrigation system like a hydroponic plant. I know that if he were conscious he'd show me the way out of drugs. Sometimes I hate him for all the poison he'd fed me over the years about the commandos, his stories about the First Lebanon War, the conquering of the Beaufort and the killing of Guni Harnik. He bottle-fed me Golani lore and took me to hang out with his army friends, who he remained close with. I had no choice but to grow up to fill his shoes.

My older brother Amir always knew he wouldn't be serving in Golani. From a young age, he always cared most of all about music. The scoliosis that forced him to undergo some difficult operations as a child scored him a poorly rated physical profile and a cushy service position at the IDF newspaper. After doing his service, he flew to New York and joined an Israeli band as a trumpet player. He returned to Israel when Dad had the stroke, stayed a few weeks, then disappeared back to his life on the other side of the world. My little sister Daphne left to find herself in a desert silent meditation retreat and a vegan diet, and Mom stayed at Dad's bedside, hoping that one day he'd wake up and pull me out of the drugs and Amir back from New York and put our messed up family back together again.

By noon, I had collected more than a hundred shekels. People were feeling generous because of the rain. I sat on the wet sidewalk on Rothschild Boulevard with my hand stretched out and a beaten metal bowl placed in front of me. I hung my head, but not out of shame. It's amazing how quickly I'd grown used to the looks of passersby and started treating begging as just another boring gig—an easy way to get the money I needed, while my thoughts were devoted only to the next hit awaiting me in my jacket cache. In my mind's eye, I was already mixing the junk on the bottom of an empty can.

A passerby bought me a hot dog in a bun with lots of mustard and ketchup, as well as sauerkraut from a can that tasted like childhood and reminded me of Independence Day celebrations. I swear, it might have made me shed a tear if that goddamn drug wasn't blocking my emotion receptors. That man really was nice. He didn't go into a whole song and dance about it, just quietly slipped the bag into my hands, along with a cold can of coke. It really was an excellent arrangement—I got a meal, while he could rest assured that his money wouldn't be used to buy drugs.

I remembered walking around with my parents on Independence Day among hundreds of people in the crowd. Mom and Dad would buy us fast food from the stalls and toys that blinked and glowed with colored lights, and we were looking forward to the fireworks. Sometimes Dad would carry me on his broad shoulders and I'd hold onto his curly hair as if it were the reins of a horse. I remember the way my father's hair felt thick and full between my tight fingers, and how excited I was to be taller than everyone else.

Now I'm treading heavily down the sidewalks that have already dried from the nocturnal rainfall, the wind freezing my bones and playing tricks on my clothes. I zip my military jacket all the way up to the neck and adjust the black woolen cap over my ears. The afternoon melts into evening, and the sunlight pales, struggling to penetrate through the clouds. I want to go back to the dump and do another hit. I can't think about anything else. I shift the corrugated iron sheet blocking the entrance to the neglected yard. The last few rainy days have sprouted wild yields of mallow, Indian goosegrass, and nettle. I can tell them apart thanks to my father, who used to take me to the fields and teach me which weeds were edible, which could be used to make tea, and which should be avoided. He was a wild animal, my father, and he knew this country like the back of his hands. He was what grownups used to refer to as "salt of the earth" and what old people called a "mensch." To me, he was all-powerful. He could do anything. Until he had the stroke that is, and after that he could do nothing.

The green cover hides the garbage the neighbors toss here. This abandoned, fenced-in area is nothing more than a dumping ground where trash and homeless junkies pile up. As I walk through the doorless opening, I hear some noise. My military boots crush gravel and broken glass scattered on the ground. I hear a growl or a purr and something like a cry or a whine, a Russian curse word, which tells me that the Georgian is in the next room. I hurry over. I have a bad feeling. I don't trust the Georgian, who isn't actually a Georgian at all, but a Russian man in his fifties, a large colossus with dark skin and coal-colored hair, which might be why people refer to him as the Georgian. His face is as hard as dirt and as cracked as the moon. He has an enormous, pointy jaw, and his narrow lips turn his mouth into a one-dimensional line, his eyes small and beady. The only reason I'm living with this thug is that all the other homeless people are so afraid of him that no one dares to even get close to our dump.

The room is illuminated with the beam of a flashlight that had been tossed to the ground, throwing more shadow than light on the walls and ceiling. I see the Georgian sprawled out on his sleeping bag. Under his left arm, held in a strangle grip, peeks out Dog's head, while his other hand is searching his backpack for something. When his eyes fall on me, he smiles and pulls out his large hunting knife, with a blade so sharp that he once showed me how sawing through eight-millimeter construction iron didn't even faze it. Though the light is murky and gray, I can see the fear in Dog's face. His eyes are nearly popping out of their sockets and his mouth is foaming.

"Hello, Mr. Geller the Illusionist, tonight's dinner special is dog," he laughs.

Dog starts fighting back, wriggling his limbs like an oversized bug, trying to bite the Georgian, but the man's arm tightens powerfully around the little neck, and all Dog can do is bite at the air.

"What are you doing?" I ask, watching him bring the knife to Dog's neck.

"I told you, I'm going to cook up some dog for us."

Nausea attacks the sides of my stomach and my heart is racing. I don't know if he truly means to eat Dog, but I have no doubt he'd kill him just for sport.

"What did he ever do to you?"

"Motherfucker was sleeping in my bag," he says, spitting at the body twitching under his arms.

"Please let him go," I plead.

"You don't have to eat it, but I kill this piece of shit anyway."

"I don't want his blood where we sleep," I try a different tack.

He considers this, his eyebrows scrunching like the elastic on a pair of underwear, but his hands still hold the knife against Dog's neck.

"This not a problem, Geller. I butcher him outside, *blat*," he says, laughing and rising to his feet, Dog dangling like a rag in his arms.

"I'll give you a hit in exchange for him," I say without thinking.

He stands before me, all 6'4" of him, Dog still twitching in his arms like a mouse in a trap, and I can practically see the wheels spinning in his head as he considers my offer. But then he surprises me by shrugging and walking toward the opening, leaving a strong smell of alcohol behind.

"Georgian," I call after him, watching his enormous body turning toward me, blocking the light. "I want that dog."

"And I want kill him, *blat*. I find him, you go find your own dog!"

I look at the poor animal trapped in his arms. It has to be a question of price.

"Two hits. I'll give you two fucking hits." I raise my voice and ask myself if it's worth fighting him over a stray dog.

He walks over and stands close to me, and I can feel the brewery emanating from his breath. I see Dog's horror-filled eyes. Something awakens inside of me—something I wanted to forget, something I pushed away. Suddenly, I find it's stronger than I am; that I have no intention of letting him kill Dog. I meet his eyes so he can see I'm not about to give up. "I want Dog, and I'm willing to give you two hits for him. It's a fair deal," I say, offering my hand. There is no tenderness and no agreement in his face—on the contrary, he hardens even more, and in the corner of his mouth I see a muscle twitching nervously, pulling a small patch of hairy cheek behind it. My entire body tenses up. I can tell that all the shit might submerge me tonight. All I want is for this big motherfucker to let Dog go, and then I've got to fix myself up with a dose. I needed it an hour ago but I tried to hold out. My shitty feeling might be nothing more than jonesing.

I watch the Georgian's hand holding onto the knife, trying to figure out if I can take hold of it before he slashes Dog's throat. My heart is racing, sweat runs down my back. I pant, trying to settle my breathing. I want to plummet to the ground, shoot up, and forget all about this.

"You give me three hits for him, *blat.*" It isn't a question, it's a statement. He pushes Dog at me, which makes the little creature erupt like a small, biting bomb, but his teeth can't penetrate past my jacket. I hold him tight, rub his head, and whisper in his ear that everything's going to be okay now, he can calm down. I sit down on my sleeping bag with him and set him gently beside me. As soon as I let go, he runs and hides under a broken chair.

"Three hits, Geller, or we eat hot dog for dinner." The Georgian laughs exaggeratedly, perhaps to make sure that I'm not about to back out now that Dog is out of his arms.

"I said two and I meant two. You'll get one from me now," I say, crossing my legs and getting the can ready.

"Fine. Two because you my friend, *blat.*"

CHAPTER FOUR

Dog doesn't move. He disappears under the broken chair and among the debris, cringing like a hunted animal in the dying light. He wants to run for his life, but he's paralyzed by fear. The Georgian's strong hands left bruises around his neck, and he can still smell him in his nostrils. He's alert to the smells and sounds, his ears sensitive enough to pick up the footfalls of a mouse in the corner of the room, not to mention the clumsy gestures of the two humans who have stopped talking. After taking a swig from the bottle with the alcoholic drink, the Georgian sits down, leaning against the wall, and lights a cigarette, the smell stinging Dog's nose. The other man rummages through his bundle and pulls out some sausage.

"Want to eat?" he asks Dog, waving the fragrant cylinder.

Dog won't be fooled again, lest he take another kick. He scoots back as far as he can, curling into a little ball of fur as if he were a newborn puppy, softening his breath, missing Zukerman.

Many smells assault him—two people and remnants of the smell of a third man who isn't currently in the room. The smells of rodents searching for food in the dark, smells that would have drawn more of his attention if he weren't so scared and achy. The man returns the sausage into his bundle, lights a fire, and busies himself with actions Dog cannot understand. The pain in his leg pounds. He folds up his tail and agonizes, licking the painful spot yet unable to bring himself any relief.

The evening drives away every bit of light, and wind whips against the branches of the adjacent tree, whistling through the cracks between the window slats. Dog feels like crying but stifles his whines. The man picks up a knife and pulls out the sausage again, slicing a piece and tossing it toward Dog, then slicing one for himself, slipping it into his mouth, and chewing slowly. The smell of the sausage hits Dog's nose like a storm he cannot resist. His feet cross the distance in a slow, excruciating crawl until he reaches the appetizing nugget, takes it in his front teeth, then flees back into his hiding place.

"You like that? I like it too. It's a poor man's supper but it keeps for weeks without refrigeration. I like sausage."

"What, now you not only try to bend spoons, but you also talk to dog, *blat*? You being, how you say, *nu*? Crazy."

"He's a mean motherfucker," the man murmurs at Dog, tossing over another piece of sausage. "It's a good thing I got here in time."

Dog can hear the man's bones creaking as he moves his limbs. He smells his body odor, but cannot detect emotions, neither fear nor joy, neither sorrow nor horror.

"It's cold today, huh, Dog? A long and exhausting summer, then boom! Winter lands on us without warning." He wrings his hands, massaging his fingers, then grabbing a blanket and wrapping it around his body. "You look even worse than I do, all ratty and neglected. How'd you end up in the Georgian's sleeping bag?" he asks, then glances at the Russian giant whose body is now folded like an exploded bridge, half hanging in midair, about to collapse. "Were you born on the street or thrown out? You must have a hell of a story. Don't we all?" He tosses another piece of sausage toward Dog and sighs.

Dog listens to the man and eats the sausage, its flavor comforting. He tries to size the man up. He's been led astray by his fair share of sweet talkers. It seems many days have gone by since that other dog bit him. When they passed him by, the man let go of the leash and yelled at the bigger dog to attack. Dog didn't manage to run away in time. The big dog caught him by the leg and jerked him around like a cat would do to a small bird. He got away by the skin of his teeth, moments from finding his death between sharp fangs.

Now this man lays his sleeping bag on the ground and slowly lies down, his head not far from Dog. He slices another piece of sausage and places it by the broken chair. "I'm such an idiot. You must be dying of thirst," he says, then sits up. He pulls a water bottle from his backpack, points a small flashlight around, revealing piles of trash, picks up some rags, turns over old newspapers, and finally finds a round plastic container that must have once contained some food. He smacks the empty container against his pants to empty it of debris, then pours some water into it and places it by the broken chair. Loud snoring comes from the Georgian leaning against the wall, louder even than Zukerman's, and filling the air in the room with the smells of alcohol and decay. The man lies back down on his sleeping bag, chuckling. "Now the moron's going to sleep till morning," he tells dog, pulling a pack of tobacco from his pocket. In the flashlight's beam, he rolls himself a cigarette. Before lighting it, he slices some more sausage for Dog, then rolls over onto his back, lighting the cigarette with an orange flame, and blowing the smoke toward the ceiling wrapped in darkness and smoke and the sounds of wind and rain. "You know, Dog, I'm so tired. It's as if I haven't slept in months. It's so sad, the state of us, being here, like this, and nobody cares."

The man's voice is soft, deep, calming. It's as if he's talking in his sleep.

"I used to be a regular person. Regular people are like regular dogs—they eat, they shit, they sleep, they fuck. They live their lives." He closes his eyes, and so does Dog. "You must have brothers and sisters, right? I have a brother and a sister, a mother who used to be a teacher and a father who's a lawyer. He used to be a high-up officer in the military, but now he's doing even worse than I am," he laughs.

Dog scratches his behind with his healthy foot, then stops because even the slightest movement hurts him.

"Maybe I was fucked up from the start, but aren't we all?" The man rests his head against the sleeping bag and blows the cigarette smoke toward the ceiling. A long honk sounds outside, a police siren wails in the distance. The man's words fade out slowly, and then he lets out a long, heavy cough. The Georgian's snoring rumbles through the room and a hard rain falls outside, its fragrance invading the room, offering Dog hints of plant oil melting into the damp dirt.

"I can't stand that Georgian with all his stories about Chechnya and all the awful things he's so proud of doing there. He might be full of shit, but I've done things that are just as bad. Believe me, I was also a big motherfucker." He lowers his voice and rolls onto his side, rolling and lighting another cigarette.

Dog watches from his hiding place. He sees very little of the man's face, only small bits in the beam of light.

"Everyone was so proud of me. They said I'm a hero, but I didn't feel like one. I was embarrassed. Ashamed. You know, Dog, I never told you, but sometimes I think staying in Shejaiya would have been so much easier than coming home. You understand what I'm saying?"

CHAPTER FIVE

A beam of light filters through the slats, stubbornly massaging my eyelids, which refuse to open. I fight it for a while, slowly sliding into a limp consciousness, then wakefulness, and I immediately feel Dog's body heat. He's asleep, curled up beside me, and though my body demands the heroin it rightfully deserves, and though I have no qualms with this right, I persuade it to wait a few minutes longer, to allow the small creature at my side to go on sleeping. It's been a long time since I've felt anyone's body heat next to me. Sometimes, at night, I can still feel the curves of Zohar's body against mine.

In Japan, she wanted to keep traveling and I wanted to go home. It was obvious to both of us that our love wasn't strong enough to overcome our desires. We could tell ourselves stories about how we were going to get back together, but I guess neither of us was the type to believe in fairytales. So we had dinner at Asakusa—a restaurant on the thirteenth floor with an unforgettable view of East Tokyo, ordered kabayaki, soba, sushi, and a bottle of sake, and shared stories like good friends rather than a romantic couple. Zohar went on to Vietnam, then to India, and the rate of her emails decreased and then stopped, but the memory of her body remained inside of me, and now Dog reminds me of her absence, the absence of a human body at my side.

The Georgian left. Before I raise my head and open my eyes, I know he's gone. There's a negative energy about that man that I can sense when it vanishes. I sit up. Dog wakes up but doesn't budge, refusing to stretch his limbs the way dogs tend to do upon waking.

I cook up a hit and check out my stock. I'm all set for today, but what about tomorrow? I've got the money I made yesterday, that could set me up for two more hits, assuming I don't buy any food.

As long as my next hit is a done deal, the whole world can go to hell. I'm aware of the strings by which heroin controls me, and yet I'm content with my lowly position. The outside world is crueler than my addiction. I wrap the tourniquet around my arm and ball my hand into a fist—easier to find a vein this way. With every passing day, with every shot, my veins disappear on me, sinking into the depths of my body. My arms are perforated like a sieve. I use a sterile pad to clean the area, and just before the needle penetrates, my heart skips a beat. A moment so beautiful it can weed out a derelict yard and replace it with a blossoming utopia. I pull out the needle, sterilize the spot again and bend my arm, cap the needle, and return the syringe to my pocket.

I look at Dog, still curled up and reluctant to wake.

"That's some lazy friend I've made," I say, getting up and walking to the armchair facing the sealed window, throwing my body against it, resting my hands on its tattered armrests, relaxed with the drug that spreads and pours and trickles through my body, flooding my brain.

I sink into the torn foam of the armchair, close my eyes, and allow euphoria to lap at the edges of my nerves like waves licking the shore. I adjust my body against the backrest and sink into the depths of a calm, quiet sea, trying to listen to outside sounds, detecting no wind or rain. The storm must have ended, but not before it filled the dump with streams of slime. The drug fills my body with the illusion of warmth. I pull out my phone, turn it on, and play the Uri Geller video. I stare at it, almost hypnotized, like watching the light at the end of a dark tunnel. The video has no sound—either its soundtrack was lost over the years or the speaker on my phone doesn't work, who can even remember. I focus on the scratches flickering on the screen. They cut to Geller's hand as it tentatively fingers a silver spoon, fluttering over it, hardly touching it, the damaged film affording the video the believable authenticity of a laboratory experiment documented many years ago. I've memorized the moment when he presents the spoon to the camera, showing its new banana shape. Then I turn off the phone and return it to my pocket before tugging on the chain holding the spoon around my neck, tug it over my head, close my eyes and search the back of my mind for the force that can influence reality and bend my spoon. I can sense it, like crude oil trapped in the belly of the earth. But if I can't set it loose, it'll never help me. I believe with all my heart that one of these days I'll open my eyes and find the spoon bending to my will.

"How's the young illusionist doing?" Crutchy Zvi asks, his statement containing a greeting, a question mark, and a sincere pleasure to see me. But he's made me lose my concentration. "Well, my boy," he says, "any news on the spoon front?" He lets out a long cough—not the kind one hears while waiting in line for the doctor. Crutchy Zvi's cough is somewhere between dying and slamming the door on the world. "A day will come when you'll perform all over the globe, just like the real Uri Geller. You'll find diamonds and oil and they'll give you a job at the Mossad," he chuckles.

I nod in agreement. I don't like being interrupted while I'm with the spoon. I'll have to start over now. I ignore Crutchy Zvi and ask the spoon to bend, loudly pleading with it to bend for me, wholeheartedly believing it can hear me, but Crutchy Zvi is listening too, chuckling and coughing up phlegm.

"I don't know what's going to come of you, Geller. From time to time when we meet I can't help but notice that your sanity is teetering on the edge of an abyss. You used to speak to the spoon silently, then in whispers. Now you and Spoon are chatting like a couple of old friends." His laughter resembles the screeching howls of a hyena, completely breaking my concentration.

I don't know if Crutchy Zvi is truly disabled, but I know he's been using crutches for the past twenty years. Maybe he had to use them after an accident and has kept them for the purpose of begging on the street. He's exactly what people imagine when they think about junkies: a mixture of drugs and time has left him faded and colorless. Life has been peeled off of him one layer at a time, and he looks like a caricature from an old newspaper that someone dumped into a puddle. All street dwellers are dirty, but Crutchy Zvi is a pile of filth with clothes on. He seems capable of disappearing inside the heaps of trash in the room, never to be seen again. His facial hair has grown savage, most of his teeth are gone, and what remains is a dark, foul maw and a bland, cracked tongue, eyes buried in their sockets like two black marbles in a barren field. He likes to speak eloquently, perhaps in order to remind me that he used to be a history teacher, and occasionally he is plagued with scholarly outbursts, attempting to pull me into an intellectual discussion, but I struggle to find the educator inside the junkie. Too many years have gone by, and the history teacher is now history.

"You've got a deceased dog on your sleeping bag, Geller," he says, causing me to give up on my attempts at bending the spoon once and for all. I place it around my neck again and slip it under my flannel shirt, then look at Crutchy Zvi, then at Dog, and then at Zvi again. He's been coming and going, coming and going, for three days now. He has a few regular spots around the city. He's the one who introduced me and the Georgian to the dump.

"Dog is asleep, Zvi."

"He's either dead or he's about to die any minute, Geller. I've raised dozens of dogs in my lifetime, and the sorry creature on your sleeping bag is not a sleeping dog," he says, leaning his crutches against the wall and sitting down on an old paint can.

I get up from the chair, bend down and touch Dog. He's warm, which means he isn't a corpse. But he won't wake up, either. I feel around his body, and when I touch one of his back legs, he lets out a cry of pain. I point the flashlight at him. His eyes are closed, he's breathing heavily, and his leg is swollen like a balloon.

"I've got to take him to the vet," I tell myself, loud enough for Zvi to hear.

"You can't afford a vet. You'd do better to share a hit with him. That way at least he'll drop dead with a smile on his face," Zvi mutters through his toothless grin, snorting with laughter. "And perhaps, my dear, only if possible, you'll share a hit with your brother, too. I'll repay you before the week returns its soul to its maker, I assure you."

"Sorry, Zvi," I murmur over Dog's head, and something inside of me shifts, like a rusty cog beginning to turn. I almost fall backwards when it hits me—Dog could die just like that dog. Then everything explodes inside my head: Dog bleeding to death, a hole in his head just like Yehoram. Dog is an Arab, Dog is a terrorist, Dog is Hamas, Crutchy Zvi's snorting laugh, the hole in Yehoram's head, his weight against my shoulder, Dog lying in a puddle of blood in Shejaiya, and all the soldiers burned alive in their APCs, just kids with their guitars and their Messi and Barça posters and pictures of pretty girls on their screen savers.

"He's going to die!" I cry, hearing myself talking, seeing the hands, but they aren't mine. This isn't my body. There's a pressure in my chest, my heart is racing, my blood shooting through me, threatening to break through valves, veins, and arteries. I pick up Dog. It's hard to breathe and my body is trembling. Dog isn't heavy, but he's positioned in a terrible dying angle in my arms. I stumble over the debris all around me. "He can't die," I mumble, hearing my words echoing through my skull, but they aren't mine. I hear yelling and I know it's Crutchy Zvi, but inside my head I hear the cries of wounded soldiers calling out to a medic. They have two parents who birthed them and came to their cribs in the middle of the night when they cried and fed them and played with them and read them bedtime stories and took them to the amusement park and dropped them off on the first day of first grade. They've got brothers and sisters, a grandma and grandpa, friends.

Outside, dawn breaks over the city, a wet and miserable dawn welded together with heavy rainclouds. I remember the vet. "Bograshov Street," I hear the words, trying to hold onto torn seams that barely hold my personality together. *Don't fall apart, not now.* But pieces of me fall to the ground and vanish between the pavement like see-through bits of skin. Fear closes in, as if I'd never shot up heroin in the first place. I put my ear to Dog's fur but can't hear a heartbeat. The sound of the exploding shells is deafening. They blow up everywhere, whistling through the air and paralyzing my body, and I know somebody's about to die. When everything explodes the Gazans die and the Hamas terrorists and my soldiers and Dog—they all die.

"This isn't Gaza, it's Tel Aviv!" I shout. The words come out desperate, like the clucking of a chicken with a knife to her throat. Even though it's morning, everything is war gray and dark and the buildings look like Gaza's buildings, and the air stinks of fear like Gaza.

"Those aren't shells. It's all in my head, all in my broken head," I repeat the words like a mantra, as if they can defeat the nightmare. I feel the drool dripping from the corners of my mouth. In war, fluids are no good—they mean something's damaged, torn, leaking. My skull is pounding. I'm not in Gaza, I'm in Tel Aviv, and there are no shells here, only a dying dog, and no one is helping, no one comes. I weep, my tears staining the road, the buildings around me as threatening as terrorist cells, full of tunnel shafts. At any moment a terrorist can pop out wearing black, carrying a Kalashnikov, shooting at Dog and me. I run, my breathing heavy and wheezing, my body sweating. The wind is cold, I'm about to die. I'm going to have a heart attack if a terrorist doesn't shoot me first. I fight not to let myself faint. I've got to save Yehoram. How I loved that kid! My signal operator is strong. He never lags behind. Now Dog feels as heavy as a sack of rocks and I limp underneath it, one step at a time, sweating my fears out of my skin, but they keep emanating, straight from the fear and anxiety factory, cracking open inside my stomach. I step in a puddle and realize I'm shoeless and my socks are all wet, but that doesn't matter now, not at war, not in Gaza. People are staring at me, wanting to hurt me. I don't know where to escape to. I'm in Tel Aviv, I know I'm not at war, I know this is Tel Aviv, not Gaza, I'm in Tel Aviv, the city of Tel Aviv. "I'm in Tel Aviv!" I scream at the top of my lungs, needing to hear the words in order to believe them. But everything is so different, and Dog doesn't feel like Dog but like Yehoram's body, but Yehoram is dead, I know he's dead. He was covering for us as he rescued the bodies from the APC, and then that motherfucking sniper shot him in the head and a warm stream of blood emerged between broken bones, and little bits of Yehoram's brain began to leak out through the cracks like red shakshuka with specks of egg white, and he fell right on top of me and I picked him up and his eyes looked at mine and in spite of the darkness I could see what one can only see in the wide-open eyes of someone who has taken a bullet to the head—a great, black, endless astonishment. So I picked him up and the radio got tangled between my legs and the bullets started whistling and I carried Yehoram's body like a bucket with a hole in it through which life was draining out. I carried him just like I'm carrying Dog now, and the whole time I thought about his mother and how she had no idea that her life was over, she was probably still sleeping, enjoying the last good night she'd ever have. In a few hours, the casualty notification officers would show up, and she'd scream and Yehoram's father would say nothing and would never speak again, because all of his words were connected to his eldest son's heartbeat, and Yehoram's brothers and sisters would lament their brother who died in Gaza, but no one would really pay much attention to their pain.

I thought about all these things as I ran with Yehoram's body, not even realizing I'd been shot, too. Adrenalin filled my body and

I was crazed, like a rabid dog. I kept running with what used to be Yehoram but had since become a lifeless lump of flesh and the bullets kept whistling by my head. I have no idea where the medic or the vet is, they need to take care of Yehoram. I run through the bombed neighborhood, and I don't want to die, and tears are running down my eyes, and I fall to my knees in the middle of the road, still holding onto Dog, and I want to raise my hands in surrender, but Dog is in my arms, and all around me is utter chaos and sirens or maybe it's just cars honking and people running and I'm crying and Yehoram and Dog are crying too, and behind me a car brakes and honks and I can't get up, maybe because of the bullet in my thigh or maybe I've got a big hole in my head from that fucking sniper who shot Yehoram, and the army is going to make the entire neighborhood shake and a ton of people will die just so we can catch that sniper, little kids and grandmas and mothers and fathers and even the boy we later found lying, legless, wearing a shirt that read "Falafel King of Jerusalem." Whole families will die and so will Dog, whom Yuval shot because he was a damn Hamas dog, a beautiful German Shepherd who didn't wear a green flag with white Arabic writing and didn't carry explosives. The dog didn't even have a beard. Maybe he was hungry or thirsty. He came over and Yuval pulled out his Glock, cocked it against his belt with one hand, and blew the dog's brains out. Then he said it was a damn Hamas dog, and I didn't do anything because it's war, so dogs die too, and it wasn't a child or a woman or an old lady, just a poor little German Shepherd, an unkempt dog, and I saw the horror in his eyes as his soul escaped through the hole in his head.

People come over from every direction. They yell and talk and touch me but I can't get up, I can't move. I hold Yehoram as he dies, hold onto him as tightly as I can so nobody abducts his body. Whatever happens—just no abduction, even if it means blowing yourself up with a grenade, don't let them abduct the body, then an ambulance with flashing lights comes to take Yehoram, but I hold him tight, wrapping both arms around him, everything about me confused, and I'm about to die. I didn't say goodbye to my mother or Daphne or Amir, and my father is lying in the hospital attached to tubes, trapped inside his head, my father who's the only reason I even joined the commando, and they'll be sad when they hear about it. They'll bury me next to my friends from the battalion. Next to Yehoram. Next to Dog.

All of a sudden, from within the inferno, pale arms reach out and take Dog, and these arms are connected to broad shoulders in a black t-shirt, covering a large chest with a golden necklace with the word "Doris" spelled on it. I look up and see that the whole thing is connected to a fat woman with a wide face, a small red nose, a million freckles, and ginger hair, and she smiles and tells me she'll take care of Dog and holds him to her chest. Those words are enough to push the fear away, and all the military memories fall away like dried mud. Yehoram vanishes in the image of Dog, Gaza is gone from Tel Aviv, a long line of cars honk behind me, I'm on my knees in the middle of the road, as if begging for my life, as if praying to God, and all around me people are talking and consulting and telling people what happened and how it happened, and I'm busy picking up the pieces of my personality from the asphalt and putting them back together again, as careful as a tightrope walker, and I let the paramedics put me on a stretcher and slip me into the ambulance; I close my eyes, and dream of shooting up.

CHAPTER SIX

Thoughts of Dog pop into my brain. I can't stop worrying about him. Has he survived? The woman who took him had kind eyes. I try to convince myself that she took him to the vet and adopted him. His leg was injured. If he got an antibiotic infusion, there's a pretty good chance he's alive. Mom always says it's good to have someone to worry about, because "when you have no one to worry about, you start worrying about yourself." I'd rather worry about Dog.

They took me to the hospital. The E.R. doctors are afraid to touch me, too disgusted. I used to be disgusted by people like me, too. The smell, the filth… It's easier to care for an abandoned Dog than a homeless junkie. I can see it on the faces of nurses and doctors and other patients and their families. They recoil from me as if I were a murderer. Their face struggles to decide what to express: fear, disgust, or curiosity. Usually, it's something that encompasses all three at the same time.

I close up like an admonished little boy, looking away and lying in my corner, waiting for the first chance to vanish. Maybe I'll grab a bite at the hospital's expense first, try to hook myself up with another hit, obviously, then slip away back to my lair. I have no identity, no name, no nothing. They don't know who I am. They picked me up off the street. I don't have to talk, I don't have to communicate.

Everybody knows the drill: they'll do what they have to do, then make me disappear, send me straight to hell from this bed that costs them a ton of money every hour I spend lying in it. The system has nothing to do with people like me anyway, which reminds me of the baggie nestled safely in the secret pocket of my jacket. From that moment on, I can think of nothing but a hit of heroin.

A nurse opens the curtain, slips on gloves, and takes my blood pressure. I don't talk to her. She asks questions and I don't answer. She shoves a thermometer into my mouth and writes down my vitals. She asks where it hurts, I don't answer. She looks at my feet. If she could, she would prefer to tend to me through a glass partition like when handling dangerous substances. She peels what's left of my socks off my feet.

"You've got cuts. I need to clean and sanitize them. You're going to need a tetanus shot, but I'm guessing you don't have a problem with needles," she says. Her words hurt me, but I don't respond. I'm still rattled by what I've just been through, a psychotic attack or an anxiety attack or some other form of madness. At any rate, it's nothing a syringe full of heroin can't fix. I want to get out of here as quickly as possible, or at least to sneak off to the bathroom and get myself sorted.

The nurse is older and worn out, and yet she seems to be making a sincere effort to be dedicated. She treats my feet. I feel no pain, just a hole in my stomach, and every cell in my body screaming for a hit.

The green curtains with the ugly print fit perfectly with the feeling of malaise. They are intended to provide privacy, but are in fact nothing but thin membranes, which any peeping tom could easily breach if they wanted to feast their eyes on the filthy creature perched upon the bed.

Hospitals remind me of my father. My father—the beloved commander and cool-headed combatant, a shrewd lawyer whose every decision was carefully weighed and calculated, lying in bed like a hunk of smelly, processed beef. My sister Daphne fusses around him as if he's got nothing but a cold, Mom is feeling hopeless but comes to sit with him almost every day, knitting him a cap or socks, reading to him out loud from the Hemingway novels he adored, but I know that, to her, he's already dead. It's like she's come to visit the cemetery, to sit at his graveside, to water the planters installed around it. Amir, who lives in New York, must still be playing music there for $100 a gig at the bars around Broadway. He's two years older than me but now looks like my younger brother. I imagine he does his fair share of drugs, but snorting a bit of coke at the club and smoking pot is not the same as shooting heroin.

On his last visit to Israel, rather than spend time with Dad, he went looking for me. By that point, I was no longer in touch with any of my friends or my old military buddies, so I wasn't easy to find. I have no idea how he finally tracked me down, but one day as I was begging for change outside of Ovad's café, he showed up. He looked like someone who'd just woken up in the middle of the night realizing they were having a heart attack. He stood there, wide-eyed, refusing to believe that the dirty bum sitting there was his brother, the commando officer.

My memory is worn out, full of holes. I have trouble tracking the timeline and placing events along it. I can't even remember if it was winter or summer, but I do remember the way it felt, an intense shame that stank like only repressed emotions stink when they rot at the bottom of your heart. He stood like that for a few seconds, then pulled a coin from his wallet and tossed it into my bowl, and the metallic sound was like a bomb going off inside my head. I wanted the roots of the large ficus to swallow me whole, to become part of the trunk behind me, my back its bark.

"Get lost, Amir," I said, dumping all the coldness inside of me onto him.

"What's going on with you? Look at what you've become! Come home."

I imagined what he must be feeling, but I could no longer stop the wheels from turning. As far as I was concerned, it was keep going or die—there was no other stop for me to get off. Of course, my brother didn't understand it. First, he said I was an egotistical son of a bitch, that I was ruining Mom and Daphne's lives. As if what happened to Dad wasn't bad enough, now I was using drugs and wandering the streets. That entire time, I kept thinking, *how dare people talk about things they know nothing about? Does he have any idea what I've been through? How can he judge me, all high and mighty, wearing designer clothes from New York, the military reporter who never spent a day in Gaza during his service? What did he know?*

Then he began to cry like a child. He crouched next to me, grabbed my hand, hard. But his tears only made my anger boil over. Between bursts of crying he said he could help me. He said that, if necessary, he would pay my way through rehab, and we'd talk to the military and the Defense Ministry and hire a lawyer.

"You took two bullets and watched your friends burning alive in an APC. There's no way in the world you aren't suffering from PTSD," he said.

But the heroin blocked my emotions and all his crying made no impression on me. All of sudden, I started finding the whole situation funny, so I laughed in his face like some mad clown, watching his mouth fall open with disbelief. It must have really pissed him off because he started cursing me out, which is when I lost my temper and told him to get out of my face before I murdered him. I made the threat sound so acute and palpable that I'm sure he almost peed his pants. Who knows, I may have really meant it. Maybe I could have murdered him.

So he left, but not before giving me a look I'll never forget for as long as I have left to live. A look that tried to be angry but contained the most horrible pain a man can feel for his brother.

Hospitals are a junkie's paradise, if you know what you're after and where to look. The nurse is done dressing my feet. They look like two little mummies. Now she stands over me, watching me with a terrifyingly pedagogical expression, as if I were a student waiting to see the principal.

"Do you want to talk? No? That's too bad. We can help you," she lies.

If you really wanted to help, you'd offer me an injection, I think but don't dare say.

"The doctor will be in to examine you soon," she grumbles on her way out, drawing the curtain behind her. I wait a few seconds before getting out of bed. I'm dizzy for a moment, my body hurts, my head is full of black nothing. I've got to get a hit. Before the doctor comes in, I've got to get a hit. I feel like lifting one of their vials, but there are so many eyes on me. I shuffle through the emergency room, and just before a nurse notices me, I close the bathroom door behind me and lock it from the inside.

Much better. But trouble's coming. Any second now, they'll be knocking on the door, and when I don't respond, they'll call security. That's how it goes with junkies—everything's preordained, nothing is more predictable than the course of a junkie's life. My life is more routine than that of an insurance agent. The regular patterns, the knowledge of what's going to happen in three or four hours. It's a perfect recipe for an anxious person who's afraid of change. The world can go up in flames and I'd still have to shoot up at least three or four times a day, begging for change, getting my coffee from Ovad, asking him to charge my phone, sitting in the armchair and watching that Uri Geller video and trying to bend my silver spoon with the force of my thoughts, and sleeping, sleeping as much as possible. When someone like me locks himself in the bathroom, it's not because he needs to take a shit.

Everything's predictable. And indeed, the knocking doesn't fail to come. The nurse asks that I open the door, but instead I open my stash, pull out the baggie, and give myself a couple of seconds just to hold it in my hand like a pawnbroker estimating the price of gold.

"I'm calling security," the nurse announces from the other side of the door. *You can call the U.N. Security Council for all I care. When I need a hit, nothing and no one can stop me. Once I take a hit I won't care anymore. I'll open the door and be as cordial as anything.*

Soldiers and junkies—both need lots of pockets in which to hide small things. The Commando cargo pants continue to serve me well. I pull out the tourniquet, the syringe, and the lighter, and search for the small dish with the short handle to warm the stuff on, but I can't find it in any of my pockets. I look up and down and forward and back, but the small dish that had turned black over so many flames is gone, which is serious bullshit. I touch my spoon, pull on the chain and it stretches into my hand—the shiny silver spoon, the one I've never cooked up in. If I use it just this once, it won't even leave a mark. I'll ask Ovad for half a lemon and polish it like a brass lamp, wash it with soap and water, and dry it well.

I'm sitting on the toilet lid in a bathroom that smells of industrial cleaner. Outside, the nurse shouts and bangs on the door, and I hold onto the spoon. As badly as I want this hit, I can't bring myself to use the spoon that has the power to save me from myself. With shaky hands, I return the syringe, the lighter, and the tourniquet to the pocket of my cargo pants and the stuff into the secret cache in my jacket, then flush, wash my hands, and open the door.

On the other side are a nurse in green surgery scrubs and a guy in an ugly hospital security uniform. I limp on my new mummy feet, passing them by as if nothing ever happened.

"You can't be locking the door," the nurse calls after me.

I climb back into the bed, not even answering her. The hospital security guard walks over with a puffed chest. Now he's going to do a detective act on me.

"Got any drugs on you?" he asks.

I stare right through him, as if he's a window. I'd tell him to be a good little boy and go back to his guard booth, but I'm too smart for that. No need to get on his bad side. He could make a fuss and call the police, and they'd send some hothead to make my life hell. I learned that 'junkie' is the lowest of all life forms, below a dog. It's best to keep my mouth shut and play pathetic.

"I asked if you have any drugs on you," the guard repeats.

I turn to face him. He looks like a good kid, probably a university student who only recently completed combat service, a little too over-enthusiastic about his part-time job.

"You listen to me now, pal. You don't get out of this bed, is that clear?" Now I know for certain he was a combat soldier. Maybe even a Golani soldier.

"Good afternoon." A young intern opens the curtain.

The security guard leaves and I close my eyes defiantly.

"So what seems to be the problem, John Doe?" he asks, looking at my chart.

I choose the right to remain silent and continue to feign sleeping.

"So what shall we do with you? If you don't talk, I can't examine you."

I feel like head-butting him.

"Look, if you don't cooperate, I'm going to have to call in a psychiatrist. And if you still don't talk, he'll send you to the psychiatric hospital. Is that what you want? I don't think so. Then you'd better play along."

Everything is known in advance. The goddamn intern is going by the book. He's just trying to scare me, puffing his chest as if he was wearing a badge of honor, sticking out his butt like Elton John singing at the Apollo Victoria, smiling with his entire greasy face and playing with his stethoscope with the self-importance so typical of young doctors. Then he drums his fingers on the bed's silver safety rail. "Still silent? Well, then I have no choice. I'll call in the psychiatrist." He throws the threat into the air and draws the curtain behind him.

The urge for heroin begins to burn a hole through my stomach.

Soon enough I'll have no choice but to take a hit. It isn't a question of if, maybe, or should, only of when—and my when is striding over at breakneck speed.

The emergency room is chaotic, people running around and partial sentences swallowing up the groans of the elderly and the moans of the ill. Something big is going on. Anyone who's ever been part of military special ops develops a sensitivity for these kinds of things, a perceptiveness of underwater currents, a hunch that orders are coming down the pipeline before you even receive them. The staff must be preparing to receive patients from a severe car accident or a terror attack. I haven't read the news in months. The only time I come across any news is when I wipe my ass with a piece of newspaper, and I have no idea if it's new or old. I find that wiping my ass against a bit of reality is even more satisfying than taking a shit.

I hear the yelling, the footfalls. Doctors, nurses, orderlies. Forces advancing and preparing to receive casualties. A few minutes go by, and in the gap between the curtain and the wall I see bloody stretchers beginning to stream in. How does the saying go? One man's misfortune is another man's opportunity. And today, I'm another man.

I get out of bed and peek out from behind the curtain. I don't need more than a moment or two to figure out where the medicine cabinet is. While everyone is busy in the trauma rooms, I cross the emergency room, pass by the nurse station and the doctors, and track down the dangerous medication cache. According to the rules, the cabinet should be locked, but it isn't. I look for fentanyl, grab a vial, and take a few syringes while I'm at it.

Now I've got to get out of here as quickly as I can. They won't be able to find me. I've got no name, no identity. They're getting off easy because I'm actually sparing them the headache of having to deal with this crap. A bottle of fentanyl and a couple of syringes is a small price to pay to not have to deal with this crap, with me, I'm the crap.

CHAPTER SEVEN

Doris had to go and shove her nose where it didn't belong and take Dog. What's she going to do with him now? She's already spent a pretty sum on the vet visit. Why does a vet visit cost more than a regular doctor's visit? Now Dog is sleeping at her house as if it's a five-star pound. All that's missing is a servant standing over him and fanning him with a banana leaf. She has no idea what to do with him. She certainly isn't planning on keeping him. She works too late and it would be abusive to leave him alone all day long. Besides, she never cared for pets—fur balls and the urine smells are not her thing. She could never understand how people could share a roof with dogs who shed on the living room sofas or cats who perch between the pots in the kitchen. Some people get really carried away and buy disgusting lizards and tongue-sticking snakes and hamsters that look just like mice. She heard some people even keep pet cockroaches, but she won't even eat dates because they look too much like those disgusting brown insects.

She decides to go looking for the young man, because she knows that for people who live on the street, a dog can be their entire universe, and she is no stranger to loneliness. Ever since her husband took off with all of their savings, and the disaster that followed, she can't remember experiencing a single moment of joy.

In the morning, Doris takes Dog out to do his business. He's feeling much better now, able to step on the injured foot. She favors this early hour. The city awakens with creaking bones, stretching languidly, yawning away the darkness, and making room for the new day. She wears leggings and a black sleeveless shirt. Even on the coldest days of winter, she suffers heat waves that race through her body, extracting gallons of sweat, as if all the anger she had for Matias has become, over the years, a reactor pulsating in the center of her body, boiling her blood.

It's chilly outside, and she grabs her mother's old umbrella—a fine object crafted with utmost attention to minuscule detail, not like the umbrellas today that work for one season before a spoke pops off or the fabric rips. Mom left her lots of things, most importantly the small apartment that saved her from going into debt after Matias took off with all her money. Like a ghost, one day he was simply gone. Never said where he was headed, didn't leave a letter. That morning, he left for his job as a salesman for a food corporation and never came home. He'd planned the entire thing in detail, even kissing her goodbye that morning and promising to get pizza for dinner.

She'd stayed up fretting all night, calling the police and the hospital, but no one was too worried about a grown man who was a few hours late coming home from work. The next morning, she spoke to his superior, who told her Matias hadn't been to work in a week. For a whole week, he'd pretended to go to work every morning. God knows where he'd been going instead. For a whole week, he kissed her on the lips, kissed the baby on the forehead, grabbed the sandwich she'd made for him, and left the apartment with a smile, humming some Carlos Gardel tune.

Their morning walk draws on. Dog is enjoying himself, stopping to sniff at passing dogs. Doris lets him take his time, never urging him, never tugging on the leash attached to the new collar she'd bought especially for him. She also pauses often to look at store windows, coveting new kitchenware or a piece of furniture.

On one of the main streets, Doris stops outside a kiosk. She asks the cashier if he's familiar with an unshaven young man who walks around with a dog just like hers, wearing military boots, cargo pants, and an army puffer coat, looking homeless.

"I think you're talking about Geller. I don't know if he has a dog, but he usually hangs out around here. I think he begs for change on the corner of Rothschild and Nahalat Binyamin, under the big tree across from Ovad's café. You know it?" As the man gives this answer, Dog pees on an electric pole.

She finds the large ficus, but no one is there. She walks around for a while, searching, waiting, pulling a cigarette from her pack and smoking it slowly, but the guy—if this is indeed his corner—doesn't show up. It may still be too early, she thinks. She is not adept in the routines of the homeless and wonders if they beg for change at regular hours like employees who have to clock in.

Dog has had enough and is ready to move on. From the perspective of his nose he senses ever more wondrous and appealing smells down the road, many poles to shower with fragrant streams of urine, countless pee marks of strange dogs that he must blur with his own. He might have the pleasure of sniffing another dog's rear-end, or even that of a female dog in heat.

But Doris won't move on. She walks over to a nearby stall and buys a hot dog with ketchup, mustard, and sauerkraut, and a plain one for Dog. Then she sits down on the curb, leaning against the trunk of the large ficus. Dog is satisfied, parking himself at her side, grabbing his hot dog with his front paws and chewing on it with gusto.

When they're both finished, she spreads her legs and pats Dog on the head. "How was the hot dog?" she asks, wiping condiments from the sides of her mouth. Dog watches her joyfully. He nudges himself into her lap, shoving his nose under her hand to signal for her to keep petting him.

"You're in my spot." The voice tries to sound threatening, as if he owns the place. But when Doris looks up she smiles, and her smile soon morphs into laughter, stifled at once by her tight fist. She doesn't want him to think she's laughing at him.

"What's so funny?"

"I'm sorry, I didn't mean to hurt your feelings." She pulls Dog closer.

"This really is my spot."

She looks him over. He's dirty, but she recognizes a startling beauty in him. "I didn't know you could own a patch of sidewalk. Did City Hall assign it to you? Do you pay property tax for it? Got a license? An insurance policy?"

He stares at her awkwardly for a moment, wondering what to say. But she beats him to it.

"You don't look like a beggar. I know you have an usual story that led you here. I'm Doris, by the way. What's your name?" She moves a red lock of hair away from her eyes, pulls two cigarettes from her pack, lights one for herself and offers him the other.

"I don't smoke these skinny kinds of cigarettes," he says.

"What do you smoke, then? Green? Purple? Blue?"

Rather than responding, he pulls out his bag of tobacco and rolls himself a cigarette. His right wrist is tattooed with Chinese or Japanese Kanji characters. He pulls a lighter from his pocket and lights up, then sits down, cross-legged, next to her and Dog, smoking.

"You don't look like a beggar, either," he says.

"I'm not."

"Then why are you in my spot?"

"I came here for you. I've been looking for you everywhere. You aren't an easy man to find, Geller."

Her words awaken something inside of him, turning his heart like dirt, and he feels tears climbing quickly up his throat, a heavy sob that really isn't appropriate right now, so he takes a deep drag from his cigarette, letting the smoke push the tears away. It's been months since a woman spoke to him, not even a sad little "hello" or "good morning." In all the months he's sustained himself by begging for change, a city or military official has never asked if he needed help, let alone who he is and what has caused him to wander the streets, relying on the mercy of people passing by. When they wanted him to enlist, they sure knew how to track him down. When they wanted him to volunteer for the Commando, they showed up. When they decided he was officer material, they located him in no time. Where are they now?

"How old are you?" she asks.

He knows she means to say he looks too young to be what he is. "How old do I look?"

"Twenty-five, twenty-six. But only because of the hair on your face and your dirty clothes. I'm sure under all that you're nothing more than a kid."

Her voice makes it clear she is neither scared nor disgusted by him. It contains no reproach. She's sitting on the curb and smokes with him like they're old friends. When he doesn't respond, she introduces herself again and offers her hand. He hesitates to touch her, doesn't want to infect her with his filth, his addiction, his loneliness. But he musters his courage and says, "Geller." He can tell by the texture of her hand that she never rests. It has a bumpy roughness formed by years of hard work.

A bus passes behind the wide tree trunk, leaving a black trail behind it, a byproduct of internal combustion.

"I love car smoke, especially on winter mornings. The contrast between fresh air and black smoke," she says.

Sure. Easy to get poetic about exhaust smoke when you have a clean home to return to.

"So what's going to happen to Dog?" she asks.

"Dog? What about him?" he asks himself more than her. "It's you," he suddenly says, his face brightening. "You're the one who took him when the medics showed up. I remember now."

She nods. Dog sits calmly by her side, resting his head on his front paws. He seems to be enjoying perching aimlessly.

"You know, I think he's happier with you."

"I work almost every day. I don't want to have a dog who's alone all the time. I treated his leg and he's feeling excellent. Don't you, sweet boy?" She rubs the furry head. "I bought him a new collar and a leash. I've got a bag of dog food at home. I wasn't sure I'd find you today so I didn't bring it with me, but I can run it over to wherever you live."

He thinks about that word, "lives," and about how he no longer has a place in which to wake up on a chilly morning in a warm bed and turn over to indulge in a few more minutes of sleep. A place where he has a razor and toothbrush and toothpaste to freshen his mouth. A place that smells of cooking and sounds of a key turning in the lock when your wife or girlfriend comes home. "I live in a dump not far from here. Just a dirty old place. I can't keep his food there, and there are other homeless people hanging out. Believe me, it's no place for him."

"Then how is it a place for you?"

CHAPTER EIGHT

I have no need to keep track of the days. Heroin is my clock, the sun and the moon that determine my schedule. Time moves between one hit of heroin and the next. I try to recall how many times I shot up since meeting Doris. That must have been yesterday or the day before, I'm guessing. The fentanyl I lifted from the emergency room is killing me, making me more sleepy than stoned. I barely got up this morning, but I didn't let myself off the hook and still spent an hour or two with the spoon. Just like every other day, the bitch refused to bend. But that's fine—I know it's only a matter of time before the spoon bends in my hand, and then I'll know I can change my life simply through the power of my mind. The moment is so close. Close enough to touch.

The heating at Ovad's is so inviting, but I honor agreements. I don't intend to scare off any of his customers. Sapir spots me and signals for me to wait. She's young and chubby and has lots of tattoos, and even though she's vibrant, she knows enough to keep her distance from me. I wait in the doorway as she makes me coffee. A few customers glance at me. Some of them know me. I ask Sapir to charge my phone because the battery is almost dead. I take the coffee and grab four sugar packets on my way to the ficus. After gathering some change, I go to the kiosk and buy tobacco, and the cashier with the dreadlocks gives me a pack of filters on the house. It's a gray afternoon, and I start feeling like a car running out of gas. I go to the dump to shoot up.

Crutchy Zvi and the Georgian sit in the dark. The room stinks, as usual, but I'm used to it. I feel the tension in the air and know they've been fighting.

"You can ask Geller, sir. Go ahead."

"I not be sir for you, retard. And you give me back the hit or I chop you like sausage, see?"

"If this is your style of conversation, I don't intend to listen. The vodka has blurred your mind, you imbecile."

"You and your stupid big words again," the Georgian huffs.

"Geller, please tell this ignoramus that I already paid him back his hit three days ago. Tell him."

"If I'm ignoramus then you are garbage."

The Georgian begins to pick his heavy body off the floor, but he's either had too much to drink or fucked up his head a different way, and before he can stand up he falls down. It seems to amuse him, because he laughs like a Lada's faulty engine.

"What's wrong, *blat*? Can't get up?" Crutchy Zvi teases.

"You no be here anymore, you hear me? If you come again I kill you. Not a good idea to try me. Tell him, Geller."

I look at them as if at two bickering children, and the only thing I want to do is shoot up. But the Georgian's threat has already pushed Crutchy Zvi's buttons, and he starts screaming like a turkey about to be slaughtered, screaming and coughing, screaming and choking and screaming some more. "The dump is mine, you hear me? I found it and introduced you to it, so you're nothing but a guest here. Do you understand what it means to be a guest? It means you visit but have no ownership and no rights, and I'm not afraid of you because you're just a guest!"

The Georgian lights a cigarette and flicks the burning match toward Crutchy Zvi.

"Why do you two have to fight all the time?" I ask, starting to prepare my hit.

"I don't want him here no more, he not a human being, he cow dung you put in ground to make potato grow faster, *blat*," the Georgian barks.

Crutchy Zvi picks up one crutch and waves it around. "The guest doesn't want me here anymore, do you understand? You're an ingrate. Do you know what 'ingrate' means, or do you need translation into Russian?"

"You read my lips, I don't want to beat you next to Geller, but if you here tomorrow morning, I give no mercy," the Georgian says, then calmly pulls out a crack pipe and puts together a hit.

Crutchy Zvi looks agitated, sad, and frustrated. Usually there's a hint of smile on his face, but now he looks like a battered animal. I've already learned not to intervene. I just want my hit and then to drown myself in the memory of Doris's words.

"Look at what a doormat I've become," Zvi murmurs as he digs through his things. "I used to be a history teacher, a history teacher in that high school, what was its name, I can't remember anymore, so many years have gone by."

The fentanyl is like a stoner superhighway. No prep needed, no can or spoon or lighter necessary. You just load up a syringe with a hundred microliters, shoot up, turn on your burners, and take off. The problem is that plenty of junkies don't know how much to take. Synthetics endurance is nothing like heroin endurance. They think if they've been taking a gram or a gram and a half a day for a few years, then a little shot of fentanyl would be nothing. They don't know it's used to put patients to sleep during surgery, and that anyone not used to it might overdose, and even those who are used to it can get dizzy or have an elevated heart rate or just stop breathing.

I'm very familiar with the stuff. I once scored a fifty milliliter vial, so we've spent plenty of quality time together, fentanyl and me. We got to know each other, and you could say we get along well.

"Get a syringe and I'll give you a hit," I tell Zvi.

He pauses in his pointless rummaging. "Really, Geller? You're willing to hook me up? What a good man you are." He sucks up to me, his voice going high like a little girl's. He finds his syringe quickly, and I fill it up with only fifty microliters. He may not be flying as high as he hopes to, but I'd rather not take that chance.

"You're a wonderful man, Geller. I wish you nothing but the best, you hear? Nothing but the best. I don't want you ending up like me or like that piece of shit over there," he whispers.

"That piece of shit is going to teach you lesson," the Georgian murmurs from within his own high. He must be feeling too good to actually get up and hit Crutchy Zvi.

I pack up my things and go to the armchair. Crutchy Zvi is on his sleeping bag, mumbling broken sentences that I can't decipher. I sink into a pleasant limpness. As far as I'm concerned, I could stay like this forever.

Crutchy Zvi has been wandering the streets for twenty years. For twenty years, he's been a jobless heroin addict, begging for change, living from one hit to the next. He has no more veins in his arms or legs. He's poked every possible spot on his body—his crotch, his stomach, his ankles. He's even shot up under his tongue. Now all he has left is the large vein in his neck, into which he shoots what was once a drug and is now nothing more than medication keeping him partially functional. If he really ever was a history teacher, there's no hint of that now. I ask myself if after more than a year of heroin use and living on the street, there's anything of that Commando officer left in me. When will I take after Zvi and drop my hygiene habits, stop brushing my teeth, stop sanitizing my injection spot? My teeth will start falling out and my skin will turn the gray-brown of dirt and fungus and infections. I live on the street, but Zvi is already part of the street. Everyone can step on him because he's part of the sidewalk, the dirt, and the dust. His humanity has crumbled, and even if someone washes him and scrubs his skin, chops off his hair and trims his nails, even if they feed him nectar and bathe him in milk and let him suckle on the breasts of a thousand fertile women, he could never go back to being that history teacher, never ever.

I sit in the armchair and look at the window as if at a view of snowy mountain. A cool breeze invades through the cracks between the slats, caressing my skin, offering the freshness of rain to air out the staleness of the dump. I try to recall how I got here, how I left my apartment, what I had before the sorrow overtook everything I used to own.

———

Doron returned from India after almost a year and was convinced the sun rose from the Buddha's ass. We would hang out in the small guest cottage in his parents' backyard in Ramat Hasharon. Most of the members of our former unit were scattered all over the world, traveling, so it was just Doron, Daud, Ido, and me, clinking glasses of whiskey in honor of Yehoram, who had been killed in Gaza the previous summer. That was his drink. He even had a tattoo of the words "Keep Walking" with the image of that goddamn Scottish lord sauntering along with his cane. So we drank the whiskey, and each of us shared what he remembered from that day in Shejaiya and made a few more toasts for all the soldiers in Sharabi's company who were killed in the APC, and a few more for all the other soldiers who were killed in that war, even though they weren't all Golani guys.

The others didn't know, but I was also drinking for poor Dog who'd come to us looking for some food and water and maybe a bit of comfort when Yuval pulled out his Glock, cocked it against his belt, and shot the poor thing in the head. Hamas dog, he'd said, kicking the body, Dog's muscles twitched because there was still a bit of life there, and Yuval's black boot was drenched with blood, painted red like a paratrooper's.

But Dog had nothing to do with Hamas, with Izz ad-Din al-Qassam, or even with Fatah. He was just a dog who happened to live in the Gaza Strip, just like the cats and moles and hedgehogs and rows of ants who lived there. Just like the birds and donkeys who lived in Gaza, and who we also sometimes bombed. Dog had no ethnic origin. He wasn't an Arab dog or a Jewish dog, he was just a poor old dog, and that's why I made a toast for him as well, then took a drag from the joint Ido had brought. It was my first time. We started laughing, and the laughing helped, and the guys from the team helped, too.

I remember suddenly telling them how I pulled a gun on the kid who ran behind me in Tel Aviv, and Doron said he thought I might want to speak to a therapist.

"The army messed with all of our heads," Ido laughed.

"That son of a bitch should know better than to run behind you in the middle of the night, sir," Daud quipped, patting my back.

"We're all messed up. Gaza messed us up," said Doron. "You can't do the things we did, see the things we saw, and not come out of it messed up. I took some stuff in India that opened my mind, cried like a baby. I spent three days crying."

"That's cause you're a pussy," Daud teased.

"Cool. I'm a pussy and you're going to keep busting your asses in reserve duty while I live it up in India." Doron lit the joint he'd just finished rolling, took a huge puff, and blew the smoke up hard, then passed it to me. "This is some good shit, sir. Not like that bullshit Ido gave you. This stuff was genetically engineered, and that's why it's much more expensive and much more power- ful, maybe five hundred times stronger than what Hendrix used to smoke. You dig, sir?"

I took a big puff and fought off the cough tickling the edge of my throat. I didn't feel a thing at first, but on the third puff I dug it real good. I felt totally loopy, jolts of electricity running up and down my body, honey dripping between the cells of my brain, and all of a sudden the world seemed much sweeter. "Fabulous," I said, leaning back against the pillow and closing my eyes. My body was loose, my head emptying up. For the first time in a long time, I felt light.

When I opened my eyes, the joint was halfway through a second round among my soldiers. Everyone looked pleased as punch.

"Hey, Doron, don't your parents mind that you're smoking in their yard?" Daud asked.

"Sitar," Doron said.

"Sitar?"

"I changed my name in India. From now on, I want you to call me Sitar," he said.

We all broke into wild laughter. It seemed to last for hours. I laughed like I've never laughed in my life. I laughed until my stomach hurt and I pulled the muscles in my face and my eyes filled with tears. I was glad to feel good. Glad that nothing was bothering me. I barely remembered the kid I almost shot in the head, and didn't mind all the people we killed in Gaza, or the fact that Yehoram took a bullet in the head and that I carried him over my shoulder with that damn radio between my legs, and I didn't think about the bullets that had sliced through my body, or how fortunate I had been, or the brain matter that leaked over my uniform, looking like shakshuka, and I didn't think about Dog, and how he twitched when Yuval shot him in the head, or even about the reserve duty we'll have to do in a few months.

We sat together until the small hours of the night. We were so stoned that at some point we just stopped talking. Infected Mushroom played in the background, everything was smoky, and there was a pile of snacks on the table. Daud kept stuffing his face with Bamba peanut-butter puffs and everyone was lost in their phones like zombies.

"Check this out, sir," Ido said, passing me his phone.

"What is that?"

"Remember that illusionist guy, Uri Geller?"

"Isn't he dead?" Doron asked.

"I have no idea, but he claimed he could bend a spoon with the power of his mind."

Of course I knew the name Uri Geller. He was considered one of the greatest illusionists in the world, but he always insisted that what he did wasn't a trick but rather a superpower. I watched the video on Ido's phone. This Geller guy was handsome, with an impressive head of hair.

"If you look carefully, you can catch him bending the spoon with his fingers. He pretends to barely be touching it, but he has this way of pushing on it without anyone noticing," Doron determined, then started searching the snack packets for something.

"Don't be dumb, Doron. Everybody knows he has actual superpowers. He's been on a ton of TV shows and he's loaded. He's got his own castle in England and a Bentley," said Ido.

"He's about as powerful as my farts," Doron quipped, lifted a leg, and let one rip.

Ido took it personally, and the two of them started to argue, but I was no longer listening. I was focused on the video that flickered yellow light from within the darkness, because all the candles had gone out, and we were all too wiped out to light new ones. I saw with my own eyes how Uri Geller bent the silver spoon. He rubbed it gently, barely touching it, and it gradually bent right in front of the camera. I leaned against the wall and decided to search myself for superpowers too. I downloaded the video to my phone because I knew I'd have to study it carefully.

CHAPTER NINE

Doris told Mrs. Peretz she'd be late. Now she looks up at the old building that must have once been very impressive. Dog pees on the fence. The place must have been designed in the Greek or Roman style, she isn't sure, with lion reliefs on the second-floor balcony wall. Now, small bricks peek from underneath peeling paint, like red flesh under skin, and bare iron bones barely hold up the broken concrete. The second-floor moldings, chiseled by an artist's hand, peek over the top of a ficus in the yard. Above them, an enormous advertisement installed on the fence promotes a new building coming soon on the ring road around the city. Dog sniffs strange pee, but stops as soon as his nose catches a whiff of the Georgian and clings to Doris's leg. He'd recognize the Georgian's scent even among a thousand others.

The weather is still cold and rainy, but Doris is hot and sweaty. She walks along the fence. If this is the place, there should be a hole. That's what Geller told her when they met and she agreed to take care of Dog—for now, she said, just for now—on the condition that he let her visit him.

She doesn't know what's so appealing to her about this guy. Maybe she's just lonely, or maybe she needs to be around someone who's in worse shape than her.

She spots an opening between two corrugated metal sheets, but the yard inside is anything but inviting. The weeds are high and bits of junk and garbage are strewn among them. It seems Dog doesn't want to go inside either, because he's pulling on the leash back toward the street. She pushes the metal sheet and Dog whines. She walks into the yard, and Dog drags reluctantly behind her.

The stench hits her as she crosses the yard and walks into the chilly dimness. This is a red flag, but Doris refuses to take heed. She tries to step confidently among broken floor tiles and debris, walking on tiptoe. She isn't frightened. On the contrary, she's as excited as a little girl going on an adventure.

She pulls on the leash, almost dragging Dog behind her. The gloomy morning barely lets any sun inside, and she waits for her pupils to dilate as she adjusts to the darkness. Now Dog sniffs around. The leash attached to his collar imbues him with confidence. He trusts Doris to keep him safe. He wags his tail from side to side and in a semi-circle. Drenched with the bold odors of rodents that inspire an appetite for prey imprinted on him by his wolf ancestors, he is as alert as a hound, but suddenly his concentration is broken by the sound of gravel crunching under Doris's shoes. Then he catches the scent of a man.

Doris still doesn't know about the stranger. She can't hear his grainy wheezing, can't smell his body, lost among the other intense aromas in the room. Dog can tell all of these apart. He's as sensitive to them as a seismograph is to the slightest earth tremor. The dark is stained with splashes of pale light. Doris doesn't see a room, walls, or a ceiling. Still, she says, "Geller?" her voice pushing against the denseness of the air, thinning out the space squeezed between the walls.

There's an armchair in front of the window, and suddenly she thinks she can sense the presence of someone sitting in it. She looks at the tattered backrest and what resembles the top of a head. She calls his name again, then takes another step forward.

Dog barks. He doesn't want her going near the man. But Doris doesn't scare easily.

"Good morning, Geller. We're here for a visit."

Dog barks. He can't tell Doris she'd better be afraid; that the man in the chair isn't Geller. So instead he pulls on the leash and pounces at the air in front of him with fierce barks.

"Enough, Dog!" she scolds, pulling on his leash in order to defeat his outburst.

But Dog ignores her. She's too important for him to stop barking, and the man in the chair drives him mad.

She tightens her grip on the leash, then tries to examine the chair more carefully. A heavy chair with high, stable armrests and a back as high as a wall. The darkness is misleading, sparking her imagination. She knows she has to be careful.

"Geller, do you copy? Over," she jokes around like a kid.

The man offers no response.

Dog growls nervously. The man's odor paints a detailed picture. Dog can tell the man is relaxed, that he's had a cigarette and a stiff drink and some sausage.

Doris wonders if the man in the chair—Geller?—is asleep or unconscious. Perhaps he isn't even alive! The thought pushes her closer.

One more step and she'll be able to see him. She hopes he's all right and has no idea why she cares. She's almost afraid to look. She knows what she doesn't want to see. She doesn't want to call an ambulance, she doesn't want to have to tell the police how she found him, she doesn't want to find this handsome young man dead or dying or choking on his own vomit.

"Surprise!" an odd figure pops up, waving its hands around like some mythical demon. Doris is so startled that she jumps back and falls over piles of garbage. Dog barks wildly, and she hears the twisted creature laughing with a rolling, throaty snort.

A beam of light illuminates her face, blinding her.

"Doris, what are you doing here?" a voice asks. A hand reaches for her. She takes it—strong and steady—and a moment later she is on her feet again. "Are you all right?"

"I got scared."

"That's just Crutchy Zvi. He isn't as bad as he looks, and certainly not as bad as he behaves," Geller whispers to her. "You're an idiot!" he shouts at Zvi. "She could have been hurt or stuck by a needle! You should be ashamed of yourself, acting like a fucking idiot."

The beam of Geller's flashlight now reveals the wretchedness of Crutchy Zvi, and Doris finds no anger toward him in her heart.

"Forgive me, madam. My thoughts got the better of me. I should have known it was inappropriate to treat a lady with such carelessness. Geller had gone upstairs to relieve himself, and I'd only wanted to give him a little scare upon his return. Can you find it in your heart to forgive me?" The fancy words and childish tone of voice softens his appearance in her eyes.

"That's my chair, Zvi. Nobody sits in my chair," Geller scolds Zvi, who gathers his crutches and hobbles over to a nearby corner, murmuring to himself.

Geller is wearing a military undershirt that used to be white. A chain around his neck carries a small silver spoon, glinting in the flashlight's beam. *He could have been so many other things,* Doris thinks.

Dog calms down and sniffs at the garbage.

"I don't want you to come here again. This is no place for you. Crutchy Zvi may be harmless, but there are others," Geller says. Rather than wait for a response, he sits down in the armchair, kicks off his shoes, and removes the silver spoon from around his neck. "Sorry, but I've got to finish my morning practice. This won't take long. If you want to wait around, we can go get coffee afterwards."

"Morning practice?" Doris asks.

But Geller has already closed his eyes and is now tentatively caressing the spoon.

"Not to worry. He lost his mind on the corner of Madman Alley and Nut Job Street. Now he's off looking for it," Crutchy Zvi says, twisting a finger against his right temple.

Doris picks up an old paint can, turns it over, and sits on it. She decides to wait a while. She's waited so long already, spending her entire life in anticipation of something that never came.

CHAPTER TEN

I wake from something that isn't exactly sleep. The buzz has worn off and my body hurts a little. The first thing I do, of course, is check on the spoon. I find it hasn't bent. My finger can tell right away that there isn't even the slightest crookedness to it. It's exactly the way it was the day I nabbed it from my parents' silverware drawer, punched a hole in it, and hung it around my neck instead of the military dog tag.

Everybody was there right after Dad had the stroke. Amir came from America, and Daphne never let go of Mom's hand. The house was bustling with visitors as if we were sitting *shiva*. Only later did I realize that sometimes death and *shiva* are better than spending years in purgatory. I was already leading a double life at that point, and no one suspected for a moment that I was a disaster waiting to happen. I pretended to care about Dad's health and joined the endless discussions and the internet research and all the hopes for improvement. The doctors knew nothing. They just said it's a matter of time and we have to be patient, but I already knew it wouldn't make any difference. Whatever happened next, our family was already ruined. Even if Dad would be able to communicate or move a single muscle in his body, what they had to look forward to from me would destroy their lives irrevocably. The spoon always acted as a kind of insurance, which is why I kept it around my neck, promising myself I'd never stop trying to bend it, because when everything collapsed, it would be my lifeline.

And indeed, everything collapsed.

Anyone else would have probably given up and tossed that spoon to hell or at the very least used it to cook up, but I know a day will come when I open my eyes and find it bent. There's no other way. Either that bitch bends or I die of an overdose, whatever comes first.

In the meantime, I want to have some coffee and maybe a sandwich, then beg for change outside of Ovad's café. I'm about to finish the fentanyl, which ran out faster than I'd expected, which means I have to go get more heroin from Yahya in his apartment in the Yemeni neighborhood, where he lies in a single bed in a smelly room, always wearing short sleeves, even in winter. On bad days, he remains lying down and gives instructions. On a good day he can sit up and pull the junk from the stash under the bed, then place it on the digital scale with shaky hands, turning it around to show me the weight is fine.

Dog's bark makes me turn my head. He lies at my feet and I recall Doris who came looking for me. And there she is, sitting on an old can, holding onto dog's leash. And she's doing something else—she's smiling at me.

"How long have you been watching me for?" I ask.

"I've had a chance to hear all about Crutchy Zvi's life, starting around the time he was ten and lived with his family in the prettiest house in Haifa, until he ended up on the street. Then he had time to go up to the bathroom, come back for his bag, and leave because he had very urgent affairs to attend to," she laughs.

I like hearing her laugh. It reminds me of a different time.

"We came to visit you. I hope you don't mind."

"I didn't think you'd actually come."

"I promised."

"Still. This isn't a place regular people want to visit."

"Does that sound like a compliment, Dog? Because 'regular'

isn't special. It's mundane. You think it's just me who's regular, or is it you, too?" Dog knows she's talking about him. He jumps up and licks her face.

"I didn't mean it like that," I say awkwardly.

"So this is where you live? Fancy. Want to give me a tour?"

"Sure," I say. For the first time in a long time, I feel like joking around. "This is the bedroom. Please forgive the mess. The house-keeper took a sick day. You've already seen the foyer. The kitchen is on the right—state-of-the-art design. Can I offer you an espresso? I have several kinds of beans."

"Double please, no sugar."

"How about a croissant?"

"I like the plain kind."

"Nonsense. I know for a fact chocolate croissants are superior."

"That's because you're sweet," she says, giggling.

All of a sudden, I feel really uncomfortable with how comfort-able I am around Doris. Something doesn't compute. No one wants to be near a junkie—no one normal, at least. So either she's totally abnormal, or something else is going on. If she's abnormal that's all right. But what if she's a friend of my mom or Daphne, and they've asked her to help me? What if Doris is just bait intended to get me off drugs? She feels sorry for me, that much is as clear as a punch to the face. An invisible crumb of pride under the cover of the drug suddenly makes me hate her.

"You've got a real dream house here," she carries on.

It's so artificial, I think as Dog pulls on the leash and sniffs at my feet. I say nothing because the thoughts are drilling through my brain and I realize there's nothing else going on here, she's just feeling sorry for me—that's all.

"Why so quiet? What's wrong, Geller?"

What's wrong, Geller? I mock her silently. Pity can drive me mad. I know she only sees my sickness, not who I used to be, just a regular guy like everyone else. "Go away," I whisper.

"What's that? I didn't hear you."

"I want you to leave now," I say louder.

"What happened to you?"

"Go away, I don't want you here." I'm shouting now and Dog starts to bark.

She looks at me, her face showing neither stress nor agitation. "I thought we were going to have an espresso with no sugar and a croissant on the side," she tries.

"Enough!" Now it's my turn to bark. I get up from the chair. "Such a nag." I pull on my military boots, leaving them unlaced, put on my jacket, and go out into the cool city air.

CHAPTER ELEVEN

Angry gray clouds clear a bit of space for the sun to light the city sidewalks with feigned warmth. A woman and a dog walk down the street. He's gripped with excitement over the discoveries pouring in through his nostrils, and she secretly hopes to find Geller under the ficus. And she does—he's on the same curb by the same road under the same large tree, Dog now sniffing around the trunk. He's holding a cup of coffee, leaning against the tree, a beat-up metal bowl at his feet containing a few coins.

"Good morning, Geller. How's work?" She smiles.

Dog sniffs at his boots, and something about that puppy nose nudge touches his heart. He pets the mustard-colored head. "You know how it is. The market is bad."

"Recession?"

"I wouldn't say that, but this isn't the best season for my line of work," he quips, offering her a cigarette.

She turns him down, pulling her own pack from her pocket.

"Aren't you cold?"

"No, I'm hot. I'm burning up. As you can see, I've got no shortage of padding." She laughs, grabbing ungracefully at her stomach fat, making it jiggle.

"You're barely dressed."

"Now you're sounding like my mother, and that's not a compliment."

"Mothers are usually right," he laughs.

"I hoped you'd be here so I could tell you off."

His laughter changes into a smile.

"You didn't treat me right yesterday."

"Sorry." He sips on his coffee and looks amused, like he's enjoying himself. "You want some coffee? I can get you some from Ovad."

"Don't change the subject. I was just trying to be friendly. And Dog missed you, too."

"Do I seem friendly to you?" he asks, not truly expecting an answer. "I'm a heroin addict. I need drugs, not friends."

She isn't moved by his words. She's got plenty of her own problems. She works hard every day. Tired people don't think as much. She spends her days cleaning houses, scrubbing toilets, sanitizing showers, vacuuming rugs, and mopping living room floors with pleasantly smelling products. But at the end of the day she goes back to her own lonely crap. "You think that impresses me?" She lights the narrow cigarette pinched between her fingers.

Dog sniffs at dried dog shit as if he'd found hidden treasure. He's delighted.

"Get over here, Dog," she rebukes.

"What do you want from him?"

"He's sniffing shit, can't you see?"

"And how are you any different?" Geller asks.

It takes her a few seconds to figure out what he means. "You're not shit. I already told you—you're just an idiot." She chuckles.

"On that we can agree."

"So what's the deal with the spoon? Zvi thinks you're crazy."

"Is that what he told you?"

"You're trying to bend a spoon with the power of your mind. Are you actually surprised he thinks that?"

He sighs before answering, as if sentenced to repeat a worn-out lecture. "Don't people go see rabbis all the time? Don't they pay money for blessings and amulets? Get coffee grain readings? Pray to God? You don't think those people are crazy?"

She suddenly recalls that after the disaster people told her to check the mezuzahs for any flaws, in case that was to blame for the bad luck. "Is that why you're called Geller?"

"Crutchy Zvi gave me that name. He's also the one who invited me to stay in the dump."

"Zvi told me he used to be a history teacher. What were you before the drugs?" Her face pushes away the embarrassment. Her eyes disclose a curiosity.

Her question breaks through a fossilized layer of estrangement in his heart, and warmth fills his chest. "Before I became a junkie, you mean? You'd never guess it. I was a Commando officer."

She covers her face with her hands theatrically. "I can't believe it! A Commando officer, how crazy!"

"And now I'm a junkie trying to bend a spoon with the power of my mind, like Uri Geller."

"Uri Geller's just a magician."

"Not at all. Uri Geller became famous because he has super-powers."

"How do you know?"

"How do you know he doesn't?"

"Everyone knows," she insists. "You're just gullible if you believe he's got superpowers. I'm telling you Uri Geller is a charlatan. It's all sleight of hand."

"You're so certain."

The truth is, she isn't. She's heard about him here and there, everyone has.

His smile tells her he's taking her silence as a victory. "I'm telling you, Uri Geller isn't a charlatan. And if he can do it, that means anyone can. It's just a question of practicing. I've got to find the right way. Here, look at this." He pulls his phone from his pocket, turns it on, and plays Uri Geller's video for her with pride, as if showing off an old friend. As she watches the video, he puts out the cigarette and rolls another one.

"So, let's say you succeed. Then what?" she asks.

"If I can bend the spoon, I can do anything I want."

"Like what?"

"Like anything."

"Then why not start with anything, then move on to the spoon?"

"I don't know why. Maybe because I already have a spoon."

"And I've got twenty spoons and my life isn't exactly a delight either, but each morning I wake up and choose to fight. I don't want you to think I'm preaching to you. You do what you want. But I realized long ago that there are no magic solutions, even if you're Uri Geller."

"You choose to wake up every morning and fight. I've had enough fighting, Doris. The last war in Gaza taught me that sometimes it's better to give up."

She can feel her heart filling with pain for him. "So that's what happened, you have Post Traumatic Stress Disorder. So where's the military? Where's the Defense Ministry? Where are your commanders? This isn't right, Geller. You shouldn't have to deal with this alone." She takes his hand, and he lets her hold it for a moment.

"I didn't say that's what happened, Doris. I didn't say anything like that. I want to try and bend this fucking spoon, and if that doesn't suit you, you can leave."

"Try and bend the spoon all you like, I've got no problem with that. Let me know if you succeed, then you can teach me how to do it."

"You're just saying that, you don't really mean it."

"Let me prove it to you. Come have coffee at my place. We can go over all the spoons in my kitchen and pick a candidate for bending. What do you say?"

"If we're going to be friends, that means you can't preach to me," he says. "Not a word about the heroin. Does that work for you, Doris?"

"No problem, Geller. You won't hear a word from me about heroin, and I won't hear a word from you about dieting, fast food, diabetes, or exercise, is that clear?"

"Clear, Ma'am!"

"Or about snacks, cakes, and donuts on Hanukkah."

"Fine. You won't bring up drugs and I won't bring up body fat."

"God, you're such a baby," she says.

They shake on it.

"Oh, and another thing—I don't want you coming to the dump."

"Didn't we just say you're coming over to my place?"

"Give me your address."

"Take down my phone number and give me a call."

"I don't have a phone."

"What'd you just show me that video on, then?"

"It isn't connected."

"I'm sure you can borrow a phone from someone."

"Fine, fine."

"Hold Dog for a minute," she says, entering her number into his phone.

Geller looks at Dog, then pats his head. "You're a good dog," he says, glancing over to make sure Doris isn't catching him in a moment of weakness. Dog is enjoying himself. He pushes his head under Geller's hand, urging him to keep patting. "Did you really miss me, Dog?" Geller whispers.

Dog looks at him, feeling Geller's hands combing through the fur on his head. There's nothing wrong with scoring a few head rubs, so he pretends to have missed the man.

CHAPTER TWELVE

The clock in Doris's kitchen says 7:30 when it starts to rain. At first it's just a few drops, almost invisible, like powder, but then with a sudden intensification it blasts down, making the windows tremble, drumming irregularly on the roofs. She'd gotten back from work in time to cook and vacuum Dog's hair, tidy up the living room, and make the kitchen and bathroom shine. She spends all day cleaning other people's homes and usually doesn't have any energy or desire left to clean her own. The notion that she was now toiling for Geller made her feel sad and amused all at once. He was homeless. He slept in a dump and begged on the street. And yet there she was, cleaning and cleaning.

After her mother died, she'd renovated the small apartment, paid the hunchbacked neighborhood housepainter to fix up all the rooms. When he climbed up on the ladder, a small man with a large hump, he reminded her of a fairytale creature. She felt bad for thinking that. He'd brought his teenage son with him, and she couldn't figure out how the son was able to miss school in order to go to work with his father. When he finished, she looked around at the fresh paint and decided that from now it would be as if she'd never even met a handsome guy named Matias.

But when her son died, it was one punch too many. Life came to a halt, and with it, her apartment. The walls, furniture, kitchen appliances and clothes all came to a halt. Everything remained just as it had been on that damned afternoon, and she was left to wallow in her defeat.

Leonard Cohen's voice fills the small apartment. Her mother used to love Leonard Cohen, and Matias used to hate him. His songs silence the thoughts in Doris's head.

A knock at the door. An almost inconceivable sound. *When was the last time anyone knocked at my door?* Last time, it was the guy from the Central Bureau of Statistics. She made up an excuse so he'd leave, too embarrassed to reveal the statistics of her life to him. Another time, it was a crook from the neighborhood who told her he was from the city's water department, but she knew him, everyone did, and knew better than to open the door.

Dog barks before the knock even sounded. Geller's scent stirs him—his tail is happy, but his ears are suspicious.

Doris opens the door, and Geller is standing there. The stairwell doesn't look much better than the dump. The building is old and peeling, and contains two apartments occupied by migrant workers, an old attorney's office, one apartment for lease, and another rented by a friendly young couple. Doris pays the building fees to the old attorney, convinced he pockets the money.

"Welcome. I'm glad you came."

"Sorry I didn't bring any wine or flowers," he smiles awkwardly.

"Next time. Come on in." She moves aside and he enters. Dog stops barking and is now sniffing Geller's feet with immense curiosity.

"Nice apartment you've got here," he says, rubbing Dog's head.

The place smells of cleanliness and lavender candles. Geller is damp with rain, and the wetness stinks of sweat, dirt, and smoke. She feels an urge to put him in the bathtub and scrub him off with soap, washing the street off of him. And the dump. And the drugs. But instead she just smiles.

"Come sit, I made us some dinner." She goes to the dining room and signals for him to take a seat. Dog follows them over and curls up in the corner. The table is small, covered in a green cloth with floral embroidery in red and baby blue. The kitchen is old but her mother's fifty-year-old oven still works perfectly, and the window is adorned with a pot of artificial flowers she'd bought at Shadi's shop down in southern Tel Aviv.

"What can I get you to drink? I've got red wine. It goes well with beef stew." She brings out a bottle and two glasses, and Geller takes the bottle and opener from her. As she goes to get the food, he uncorks the bottle and only pours wine into one glass. He used to love drinking. He drank wine on dates, beer with his friends at the bar, and anything that was offered to him with his army buddies. But ever since he started shooting up, he's avoided alcohol. Both substances suppress the central nervous system, and the combination could cause him to sleep for a full day.

He watches Doris stirring the pots on the stove. Her hair is a red mane, followed by a bit of neck, broad shoulders, fat rolls around the waist, and an ass squeezed into black leggings. As always, she wears a sleeveless shirt tightened around a large bosom. She takes the glass of wine from him and doesn't ask why he didn't pour himself any. He tastes her food, beef stew with potatoes and mushrooms.

"Delicious," he determines. He fills his glass with water and they toast. "So you live on your own?"

"Ever since Mom passed away."

"Husband? Children?"

"I used to be married," she says. She's got a lot more words than that, but her lips seal up and her tongue stirs around inside her closed mouth. The wine pushes the words down.

Geller keeps digging through his plate, and she gets up to serve him seconds, but he knows his stomach isn't accustomed to large portions anymore, so he signals for her to sit down.

"So, Geller. Tell me how one goes from Commando officer to street dweller and drug user."

He sighs. He knew he'd have to offer something in return for this invitation. But he's not about to play this game. "Just like people go anywhere else," he finally says. "They start walking and the road leads them there. But honestly, I'm not in the mood to talk about it."

Doris empties her glass and refills it. She likes to drink, but has forgotten how to do it with another person. Her head starts to feel happy, so she gets up and grabs an ashtray from the kitchen windowsill and a pack of cigarettes from the counter. When she sits back down she lights herself a long, thin cigarette.

"Say, Geller, what do you do when you're totally alone? I mean, what kind of weird things do you let yourself do when no one's watching?"

"I roll a cigarette," he says, rolling himself a cigarette.

"Come on, be serious."

He's amused by the fact that she's tipsy, so he lets himself say, "I used to mimic famous people's faces and look in the mirror to check if I looked like them. One of my favorites was Adolf Eichmann. Remember what a crooked mouth he had?" Geller twists his mouth to the right.

"You look like you just had a stroke," she laughs, not knowing how much that hurts.

"Your turn," he says.

She drinks a little more wine and smiles, embarrassed. Leonard Cohen's voice is soothing, reminding her of her mother and poking Matias in the eye. "Well, okay, but promise you won't laugh," she says. Without waiting for him to promise, she continues, "Sometimes when I'm in bed, I slip my hand into my underwear, grab the hair down there, and pull. Then I count how many I pulled out and hope to find more than seven."

"Kinky," Geller says, chuckling. Her intimate confession takes him by surprise. He feels so small next to her.

"We said no laughing!" she protests, tapping her cigarette over the ashtray.

But embarrassment has him asking, "Why seven? Is that your lucky number?"

She doesn't tell him that her son was seven. Instead she takes another sip of wine.

She says nothing, and he has to make up for laughing, that much is clear to him. So he confesses, "There was this thing I used to do when I got home from high school. I'd pretend I was in a SWAT team entering a building where terrorists were holding hostages. I'd stand in the doorway, count to three, and then go in shooting, killing the terrorists and releasing the hostages."

"Sometimes I sit in the living room and pretend I'm being interviewed on the news," Doris offers drily.

"What's the interview about?"

"How I murdered Matias."

"Matias?"

"My ex-husband. He stole all my money and disappeared."

"Son of a bitch." Geller leans back and adds, "I can understand that. If I were you I wouldn't just imagine it. I'd kill him for real."

"Good riddance," she murmurs.

"So he left you all alone?"

"With debt." She pauses, then adds, "And a baby."

Geller glances around, sensing something, but also sensing this isn't the right time. He notices Doris's foot bouncing and her left hand balled into a fist. A hard rain blends into Leonard Cohen's singing. "And you have no idea where he disappeared to?"

"Must have gone back to Argentina." She rests her chin on her hands and looks at him. "You're a handsome kid, Geller."

It's been a long time since anyone's complimented his looks. Zohar used to like his face. She said he looked like an old-timey Hollywood movie star.

All of a sudden she says, "You want to take a shower? I threw out all of Matias's clothes, but I might be able to find you something."

He gets up, ignoring her offer. He takes a few steps toward the living room, then returns to the kitchen. His mind plays tricks on him. She can't be lusting after him, hoping to get him into bed after he steps out of the shower. He isn't the man he used to be. He's filthy and smelly and mad. No one would want him. And she's old enough to be his mother, goddamn it. "Actually, I think I'd better go. The rain stopped and I need to take my medicine."

"You can take it here, I don't mind."

This surprises him, and his surprise instantly transforms into recoil. "Thanks," he mutters. "Maybe another time." He gets up and walks to the door. Dog rushes over.

"I don't want anything from you," he hears her say behind him as he stands in the doorway. "Just don't disappear on me. Can you promise me that, Geller?"

"I'm not going anywhere, Doris," he says, closing the door behind him before she can see him crying.

CHAPTER THIRTEEN

I hear a wolf howling. It's distant and tormented, extracting thoughts from their burrows, where they scan the abysses in search of foggy shards of memory. I look up toward the large windows. My head is so heavy I think my neck won't be able to carry it, and it might detach and roll away like a bowling ball. There are no wolves in Tel Aviv, at least not the furry kind. The windows are dark, just a few lights twinkling behind them. A wolf in the heart of Tel Aviv? I must either be too high or not high enough. The wolf is probably just a dog who lives in my head. The windows are closed, probably sealed shut, and there's no chance I could have heard any howling all the way up on the fifth floor anyway. Still, I go to the window to take a look outside. The darkness reflects my own face, which I don't want to see—the stubble that has hardened with dirt and clumped together with tassels of filth, my eyes which are as extinguished as the coals of a dying bonfire. I also see the white plasticity of the room, and my father, trapped in the hospital bed like a potted plant.

I turn around and look at him. I'd never have guessed he's a vegetable. His eyes are open, his pupils flickering occasionally. He seems to be aware. His lips part lightly, revealing yellowing teeth. Do they brush them daily? Do they maintain his body? How long will he continue to lie around like that, staring into the void? He's lost so much weight he looks like he just had gastric bypass surgery, like he has cancer, like he's a junkie. He used to be a big, broad man, a Golani signal operator. Golani soldiers have fought in all of Israel's wars and the Golani Brigade is one of the IDF's most highly decorated infantry units, often one of the first brigades to be called to reserve duty. My father was in the 51st Battalion, also known as the Groundbreakers. Then he was an officer in a Commando unit. I think he respected Arabs but never trusted them, he claimed there would never be peace. He didn't like left wingers much either, but he loved the military, loved Golani, and loved the country.

I sit on the chair by the bed and look at him, just like I've done every other time I've visited him over the past year. I've always just looked at him and never tried to talk. The doctors said talking could help, and so could playing music, singing songs, even showing him pictures. And, of course, the most important thing is touch—holding his hand, caressing him. Mom used to play him Shlomo Artzi songs, mostly "Restless Night." He loved that entire album, and especially that song. She would play it twenty times in a row, as if it were some magic potion. Daphne caressed him like one caresses a baby, like he used to do to her when she was little. She held his hand and whispered to him to wake up, to go back to being his old self again because everybody missed him so much. Amir was out of the country, so sometimes he just shouted at him through Skype. I came over for comfort. It was like standing next to the rotting trunk of a tree that used to be formidable. You could still be impressed by what he used to be, feel sad about what's become of him, and think about how we're all mortal and how, right now, you're in much better shape than he is.

The doctors said that nothing was likely to help at this point. They had statistics. It would take a miracle. I don't believe much in miracles, and even if I could wake him up, I'm not sure I would. Now that everyone had gotten used to things, it seemed kind of unfair. Besides, he was the only person I could visit without worrying about endless arguments, preaching, or fights. The trick was to show up when Mom and Daphne weren't around. If I caught wind of them being there, I took a step back because I couldn't bear the sorrow in their faces. At first they tried everything they could to bring me back to normal life, but now they've given up.

Even if I live fifty more years, I'll never forget my mother's face when she realized I was using heroin. I don't think she realized, even then, how deep of a hole I was in. She was still busy processing everything going on with Dad, and then I came at her with the heroin. Life hadn't prepared her to deal with a sequence of disasters, but she tried—I've got to give her credit for that. One day, she told me she'd spoken to a therapist who explained that if a junkie didn't want to help themselves, no one in the world could ever convince them to seek help. That's exactly what she told me, and then asked me not to come back to the house again, and said she wouldn't be giving me money for drugs anymore.

A family can fall apart like a Jenga tower if the wrong brick is pulled out. One moment everything's fine—well-adjusted children, happy parents. The kids are out of the house and the parents can go off traveling the world just like they used to dream of. The next moment, everything falls apart on you.

Dad's eyes watch me. I have no idea what they see. He's no longer really my father, just a complicated package of organs.

I remember how Dad used to keep a licensed revolver in a shoebox on the top shelf of his bedroom closet, under a pile of shirts he hardly ever wore but still held onto. Beside it were a few photos from different moments along the years, and love letters Dad had written Mom when they were young. I read them once and thought to myself that the man in the letters and old photos couldn't possibly be him. *This can't be my father, the lawyer, the combat soldier, the tough guy who always knows how to cut to the chase and keep his head straight.* But I discovered he used to be a romantic who wrote poems for his lover. He kept the revolver and the love letter in the same place.

I don't know why I keep visiting. There's no chance of him waking up and no chance of me stealing anything because the entire staff knows I'm a junkie. But they have no choice, they've got to let me in, so they take the elevator up with me and lead me through the hallways and into his room. They don't let me wander. I spend two or three hours with him, just looking at him and hoping no one else shows up. Every so often I touch Uri Geller's spoon and think about how life is destined to end, and the only question is how you leave and how much dignity remains when you do.

His eyes are still blue, but something about their blue has changed, like the way the color of the sea blurs and turns murky with sand. His eyes are buried in caves of bone, sunken, drowning in the traces of his consciousness. His skull is revealed by the receding of his hairline, and wrinkles spread violently over his face. He seems to have aged twenty years. He looks at me but sees nothing, and I wish he did, wish he'd put his arms around me, startle and shake me and hold me with his large hands and clean the drug off me and make me a proud fighter again, a combat officer.

Poor thing, I think, not sure if I'm referring to him or myself. I usually avoid crying around him, but now it's happening, totally unexpected. I think the tears come before the sobbing, which is odd because I always thought it was the other way around. For the first time, I find myself holding his hand and crying. I'm not sure how long this goes on for. I can't ignore the crying and the feeling it gives me, of a desire to get cleaned up and get back the life I used to have. But that feeling is weak, almost imperceptible. I hold onto it for a moment, but it slips between my fingers. It's like trying to hold onto the wind.

The longing for the drug puts an end to the tears and everything that comes with them. I don't want anything anymore, except to shove a needle into my arm, to feel the stuff pushing its way into my vein, flooding me. I place Dad's hand on the bed and rush out of the room. I don't say goodbye to him, don't kiss him, don't caress his face. My body is filled with purpose. No more crying and no more nonsense. I need a hit.

Even though its early evening, daylight savings and the cloudy weather have made it dark outside. At medic training, I was taught to track down veins and arteries at any time, place, or weather. My heart flutters its wings. The son of a bitch knows he's about to get his fix. I can't see anything around me, can't hear or smell. I'm locked onto my target. I'm sitting on the bus, but my mind is on that empty can and the lighter's flame and the thin needle and the small filter, the junk swirling in tiny bubbles as its sucked into the syringe, the logistics of molecule transfer into the brain. I want to sink into the pleasant feeling that shuts me out of my surroundings and my memories and myself. I want to forget everything, just for a few minutes is long enough.

Tel Aviv moves beyond the large bus windows. I'm reflected in them as my father was reflected in the windows of his hospital room. My image is mottled with tiny droplets of what hasn't ripened into true rain but is sufficient to dot the window and cover my skin with blisters that ooze all over my reflection. A sour urine smell fills the bus. Perhaps it's coming from me. I cringe awkwardly in my seat. That's encouraging, the fact that I can still feel awkward. I'm sure Crutchy Zvi no longer feels awkward. I can picture him sitting in my place and letting a rumbling fart rip as if he were alone on the bus. The people around me pretend to concentrate on their mobile phones, the music in their earbuds, the book in their lap. But I can sense the looks they sneak my way, more curious than scared. Their eyes are like clicking tongues.

When I get off at the station, the rain showers down with purpose, and I zip up my jacket and pull on a cap. I see no cars, no pedestrians, no buildings, and no city—only my military boots stomping through the dark, because there are no streetlamps here. I walk into the dump's yard. The high weeds kiss the ends of my pants with cool dampness, and I step among them, looking up. No stars and no moon, just the thick fog of rainclouds. All of a sudden, a cry cuts through my thoughts, and my body operates independently. My feet hurry into the collapsing building, take a left into the dark room. And I don't know how I recognize them, since their bodies must be darker than darkness itself, but my hands find his jacket and I pull on it, and I hear her, and punch him in the gut, and I punch him in the face, and I feel him falling to the ground, and then I hear her heavy breathing.

"I wasn't doing anything to her, *blat!* Why hit me, Geller? Why hit?" the Georgian cries. My nose catches a strong whiff of vodka mixed with the smell of blood—salty and metallic and full of death.

I don't respond. I refill my lungs with air. I'm so angry I kick him in the stomach and hear him moaning and cursing in Russian. Then I find Doris's hand and pull her out with me. I've got to get out of here because I'm suffocating, because my hands are liable to kill the Georgian, because a missile can shoot through these windows at any moment, breaking down the slats and blowing us to smithereens.

"Are you all right?" I ask. "Did he hurt you?"

"He just scared me."

I'm glad to realize the blood I smelled came from him; the punch I gave him. I'm going to have to be careful. The Georgian is insane, dangerous, a terrorist.

"Come on, I'll take you home."

CHAPTER FOURTEEN

Dog's tail wags with a force that threatens to knock him down—a motion tied by an invisible thread to a pleasure center and automatically switched on whenever he is joyous and excited. He hops around on his back legs in a sort of ludicrous drunken dance. His front paws scratch the door, and he can't help but let out the barks that emerge from the depths of his heart.

He's in love with Doris. He loves her so much that the memory of Zukerman almost fades away completely. He loves the odors her body emits, her soothing voice, and her embraces, which always end with fur pats and head rubs. He loves the way she gently takes hold of his ears, and how her fingers burrow through the delicately pleasurable spots behind them. He loves her kisses, which he returns by licking her face, neck, and hands. He rolls onto his back, and she scratches him in spots that put secret wheels in motion, moving his legs around as if they were pistons rather than parts of a living body. She's his entire world. She loves him back, gives him food, plays with him using a fragrant bone and a ball, takes him on walks all over the city, and now she's home again. He hears her footfalls and smells her behind the door. She's not alone. He's so happy he can't be bothered to sniff at Geller, who supports her as they walk into the apartment, seating her down on a kitchen chair and boiling water in the kettle.

She reaches over to Dog and rubs his head, and only then, once he's settled down a bit, does he smell desperate fear on her and the wagging of his tail dies down in an instant.

"I was so worried about you," Geller says after finding cups and a spoon and powders to mix with the water.

"I'm fine. Nothing happened."

"You're shaking. What did he do to you?"

"He didn't get a chance to do anything. You showed up in time." Her words are weak and weightless, floating out of her mouth like fog through the air.

There's a pack of cigarettes on the table. She pulls out a skinny cigarette and smokes it with trembling fingers, listening to the spoon rattling in the mugs after the water boils. Geller carries the mugs to the table and sits down next to her.

Dog sits on the floor between them, supposedly doing nothing, but in fact letting his senses track the events carefully.

"You should file a police report."

"But he didn't do anything. I already told you, he didn't get a chance to. He just said a few words and then grabbed me, and then you came."

"What did he say?" His body coils.

"It doesn't matter. I don't want to repeat it."

Geller is upset with her for going over there by herself. If he hadn't made it in time… he doesn't want to think about what might have happened. "Please, Doris, don't go there again. It isn't safe. My world isn't safe."

"Is it safe for you?" she murmurs.

Geller isn't comfortable with the question. His mouth opens, then closes. He shakes his head in a gesture implying that he doesn't know what to do about this stubborn woman. He takes the coffee cup between his hands, either to drink or just to warm up, then takes a long sip. The beverage slurps between his lips in a whistle. She looks at him for a moment, then lets out a liberating laugh, a long laugh that contains all the fear embodied in her, a laugh that has a clear beginning but no predictable end. But she stops laughing when she notices his hand is injured. He must have cut himself when he punched the Georgian.

"Your hand's hurt." She takes his hand in hers and examines it under the kitchen light. Then she lets go and walks over to the bathroom. "Come with me," she says.

"I'm fine," he says. "It's nothing." But he follows her, and Dog follows him.

"Doesn't it hurt?" she asks, digging through the medicine cabinet.

"Doris." He stands behind her, sounding for a moment like the commander he used to be, meeting her honey-toned eyes in the small mirror. "I'm sorry, but I really have to get my fix." His voice dies down. She smells of shampoo and body wash, and he, on the other hand, is filthy like a wounded animal. He's impure, he's rotting juices, injured and bleeding, and he's got no more words, all memories draining into the cuts on his hands and the veins begging him to stick a needle in them.

Dog watches alertly.

"I've got to shoot up."

Her hands stop rummaging through the medicine cabinet and her eyes return to him. She turns toward him, and he closes in on her like petals, smelling of cigarettes and of the filth that clings to him like pollen to a bee's legs. "What's your real name?"

"I don't have one anymore. You can call me Geller, just like everyone else."

"I want to know your real name," she insists.

"The person I used to be doesn't exist anymore. Now there's only Geller."

"You have such a beautiful face, my child."

He doesn't answer. Only closes his eyes as she runs her thick fingers over his stubble.

"Look at me," she pleads.

But he doesn't dare. If he looks at her, he might cry like a child, and he's not a child anymore. Not even a soldier.

"Take a shower. I'll find you some clean clothes. Get cleaned up, lie around in the tub for a while. I can help you. Really." Her lips are close to his. She talks like a mother wishing to protect her son, but her body says something else. Her lips are red, her breath sweet. For a moment, he's the man he used to be again.

He's got to shake the feeling off, so he mutters, "I don't need any help."

"Everybody needs help. You're no better than others."

He knows exactly where she's leading him. He tries not to be insulted. He knows she means well. But right now, the only help he's yearning for is a syringe full of heroin.

"Stay with me tonight, please, Geller. I'm frightened."

Before he responds, his hand feels around the outlines of his pockets to track down the syringe and the baggie. "I'll stay with you tonight," he says drily, "but I've got to shoot up." A part of him wants to stay, to inject his medicine and sink into Doris's hot bath. The other part of him wants to go back to the dump. To what he's used to.

Her eyes say what her mouth doesn't dare. She wants to tell him to stay and not shoot up. She wants to say that she'll take care of him like she would her own son. "I already told you—you can shoot up here. I understand the situation. I'm not some fairy godmother from a storybook that can wave a magic wand and make your addiction disappear. So I want you to feel comfortable. To feel at home."

He doesn't know what to say. He makes do with a nod.

"Take a bath. I'll get you a shirt and pants from the closet. I'll wash these clothes for you real quick." She plugs the bathtub and turns on the hot water.

After she leaves, he makes sure the door is closed, sits down on the toilet lid, and gets himself set up. The heroin almost spills out of his shaking hand, his veins are screaming, his heart racing. The flame licks at the small utensil, warming up the drug. He doesn't feel good. Maybe it's the warmth of the place, Doris's big eyes, the hot water climbing up to fill the bathtub like a swelling reminder of everything he left behind, everything forgotten and irretrievable.

He fills the syringe and taps it with his finger. The tourniquet is wrapped around his left arm. He opens and closes his fist, and large tears crowd the corners of his eyes, blurring his field of vision, confusing his thoughts. His blood is bubbling, and he has trouble figuring out where all these tears are coming from all of a sudden. Heroin takes the edge off, arranging his memories in a hidden archive in the back of his brain, but something has been breached, letting loose the tears, which are now streaming down his cheeks. He feels around his arm, searching for the bump of the vein. They taught him how to insert an I.V. line in the dark, when all around him tracers painted red stripes along the sky and bullets whistled by his ears. They taught him how to kill, but also how to save a life under cover of dark. The needle penetrates. He takes a breath, then presses down on the syringe, pushing the stuff in. He loosens the tourniquet, bends his arm, wipes away the tears. He's feeling much better now—the cells of his body, which had been screaming like a billion hungry babies, are now satiated.

He rinses the syringe in the sink and clicks the plastic cap shut. The water in the bathtub is steaming. He turns off the faucet and takes off his jacket, shirt, and military undershirt. He looks at himself in the mirror, but his reflection is foggy. He pulls off his pants, embarrassed by the color his underwear has taken on from his body, the smell emanating from it. He doesn't want her touching it. Doesn't even want her seeing it.

He steps into the hot water, which stings his feet, ankles, and shins. He squats down and the water tingles his testicles. The pain feels nice, reminding him he's got a body. The burn reddens his skin and awakens human emotions. He sits down, holds onto the sides of the tub, and lies back, cooking in the heat, closing his eyes so as not to see the filth transforming the water into a murky puddle, all those months on the street washing off of him. His heart is racing, and only when he feels a hand atop his head does he open his eyes and realize he's crying, and the tears mix with the water, the hand feels good, and he watches as she grabs a sponge and bathes him gently. He can't stop her, and for the first time, he doesn't want to.

Outside of the bathroom, Dog sits down on the couch. He rests his head against the gray cushion. Even with his eyes closed, he's aware of his surroundings. But for now, he allows himself to nap for a bit.

CHAPTER FIFTEEN

"Do you mind if I give you a shave and a haircut?" Doris asks.

I don't mind. I'm willing to surrender to her. She picks up scissors and a comb and chops off my hair. She's got good, steady hands. Her body turns pink in the heat of the steam rising from the bathtub. She's wearing a gray undershirt and her large breasts move underneath it, I watch them as if they were a pair of hypnotists. I close my eyes and she works on me thoroughly, not talking. All I hear is her scissors going shlak-shlak as they shuffle up my hair.

"I want to shave you," she determines. Who am I and what am I? A patient cannot refuse a doctor's orders, and I'm a dying man. I'll agree to anything she asks and do anything she wants. I hold onto my Geller spoon and squeeze my eyes shut to keep the tears from coming. Dog scratches at the bathroom door as the scissors have their way with my beard. Her fingers grab at locks of my hair, the blades cut, and the hair falls and my eyes are closed and my heart pumps blood powerfully, like an industrial pump using up the remains of its juice before giving up.

"You already look so much better." Her voice reaches me as if from a different planet. A moment later I feel her anointing me with shaving cream, then running a razor over my face, the blade sharpening me as if I were a whetstone. From time to time, she taps the razor against the side of the tub to remove the hair caught in it.

"Look how handsome you are!" she cries, offering a hand

mirror. And I try to see beauty, and what I find is large eyes, green like the uniform I used to wear, thick eyebrows, a prominent nose, full lips, and cheeks as smooth as a teenager's. I see all of these, but I can't imbue them with a clear personality. They are as foreign to me as a yearbook photo of a person I've never met. I ask her to leave me alone, and she walks out of the room without protest.

The water has cooled and my skin is covered with goosebumps. I sit up and pull out the bathplug. The blackened water drains, carrying away memories that stretch and distort until they disappear into a small, dark hole. I wish it would pull me in with them, to disappear in underground pipes. My body is still dirty, so I scrub it until my skin turns red, then rinse myself with scalding water. After that, I stand up and clean the bathtub of hairs and the grimy line delineating the level of my filth on the white ceramic, leaving a clean tub behind me.

Doris left me a soft towel. For a long moment, the water drips off of me and onto the red bathmat. I don't dry myself, just hug the towel to my body as hard as I can, as if it were every soft and sweet thing in the world. When I finally wipe myself dry, I find that in spite of the soap and water there are still dirt stains on the towel. It seems that in order to clean all the filth off of me, I'd need to be soaked and boiled and bleached. The layers of filth that had accumulated on my skin for months cannot be removed with a single bath. I toss the towel into the hamper and put on the clothes Doris left for me—long sweat pants and a man's white undershirt. I pull on socks that resemble colorful marmalade and breathe in Doris's warmth and fragrant laundry detergent.

I step out of the bathroom, pulling hot steam behind me, as if I'd just opened the door to a sauna. Dog welcomes me with a wagging tail.

"Your clothes are in the laundry and I'm heating up some food for you," Doris says, peeking from behind the kitchen door.

"Thank you, Doris." I walk over.

She takes my hand, and I let her lead me to the dining table. I watch as she serves me a large schnitzel and a bowl of red rice. She's already sliced a tomato and a cucumber and arranged them in fans on a plate. Now she smiles at me with satisfaction and anticipation of watching me eat.

I begin. The kitchen is bathed with warm light, the fridge rattles softly. Dog watches me pleadingly and occasionally lets his tongue hang out. I look at Doris, her small apartment, the possessions she's accumulated. I finish chewing and think that maybe there is still beauty in this life. I swallow down a final piece of schnitzel and notice that I'm feeling good.

"That was delicious," I say.

A smile shines upon her lips. Dog shoves himself between my legs and rests his head on my thigh. His eyes are longing.

I sip on a glass of Coke, welcoming the burning of the bubbles and the sweetness of the sugar, which lifts the heroin high a bit. We light cigarettes and smoke like two normal people. If I could, I'd ask for this moment to last forever, for me to never need my next hit, to be able to return to life. I know that within a certain amount of time my body will be screaming like a hungry baby again, and yet I smile like a fool until Doris crushes her cigarette in the ashtray and carries the dishes to the sink. A few moments later, the smell of Turkish coffee fills my nostrils.

"Yehoram used to make us the most amazing Turkish coffee," I say mindlessly.

"Yehoram?"

"Yes, Yehoram. He used to make the best coffee I've ever had."

"What happened to him?"

"To who?"

"To Yehoram," she says, her words mixing matter-of-factly with the coffee.

Some noise is driving me mad. It's like a tiny person banging a tiny hammer against the wall. For a moment, I think the banging is just in my head, but then I spot a beetle on the table behind the saltshaker. It bumps repeatedly against the wall, trying over and over again to break through. "It's a long story."

"Luckily, we've got time," she says, removing the coffee from the stove and pouring it into two small, thick glasses.

"After I got back from Japan," I mumble.

"You're rushing ahead, I'm not following."

"After military service, I went to Japan with Zohar, who used to be my girlfriend. I came back alone because Zohar wanted to keep traveling and we realized that said something about our relationship," I tell her, wrapping my hands around the coffee cup.

"So you came back alone."

"Yeah. And then my dad had a stroke."

She grabs my hand and squeezes.

"He's a vegetable now." I suddenly let out a meek laugh.

She says nothing, but her hand keeps squeezing mine.

"It's a shitty story, he didn't deserve it," I find myself saying. "He's been hospitalized here in Tel Aviv for months, in a consciousness rehabilitation ward, even though there's no chance of him rehabilitating. It shocked the family because he used to be such a strong man, my father. A lieutenant colonel in Golani. After he was honorably discharged, he studied law and started his own firm."

"You must have looked up to him," she says. The beetle continues to slam itself against the wall pointlessly.

I knock the beetle to the ground, and the banging in my brain stops. "My entire life, I've done my best to be a winner for him." I add four sugars to my coffee. She must wonder how much more poison my body can handle. If she wasn't looking, I'd add another spoon or two.

"Is that when the nightmares began?" Doris asks, as if I've already told her all about how Yehoram was killed in Gaza. She gets up, picks up the coffee pot, and rinses it in the sink. "Keep talking, I'm listening."

"I couldn't sleep. I'd wake up from bad dreams. I couldn't function.

All the dead of Gaza haunted me everywhere. I shot and bombed and killed anything that moved, commanding children and sending them off to kill, and those damn terrorists emerged from every hole in the ground like moles, launching missiles at us and shooting at us. My friends burned alive right in front of my eyes, and then Yehoram got a bullet in the head and his brain leaked all over my uniform." I feel anxiety rearing its ugly head, take a deep breath, close my eyes, let the air out slowly, and try to relax.

"You're here now. You aren't in Gaza," she whispers maternally. I feel her hands on my shoulders. "Then why didn't you go see the military psychiatrist? They must have a department dedicated to shellshock. You could have received a disability allowance. You're a hero, Geller. Do you understand what a hero you are? They can take care of you. They have to."

"They're good at destroying, not repairing."

Doris sits back down, taking my hand again.

"It doesn't matter now," I say.

She looks at me, her gaze compassionate, and her eyes glazed with tears. She feels my pain. Bit by bit, I relax. "Well, you stay here with me for as long as you want, you hear me? As long as you want. You don't have to go back to the dump. I don't want you going back there."

"You're sweet, really. And I appreciate all of this. But I can't drop all my shit on you. You've got your own life and your own problems. You don't need my trouble."

"Don't you dare call yourself trouble," she protests. "I'm not about to argue with you. You'll sleep on the sofa, end of story!" She makes the decision for me, and perhaps that's exactly what I needed.

"As you can imagine, I've slept in worse places," I laugh.

She gently touches my palm. "How's your hand?"

"My hand is fine. I don't feel a thing." I pull it away from her. "And how are you?"

"I've got a new toothbrush in the bathroom, you're welcome to use it." She evades the question and I don't insist, nodding my head.

Once Doris goes to bed, I'm once again nothing more than a junkie that she let into her home. There are linens, a pillow, and a blanket on the sofa. I smoke another cigarette and brush my teeth, indulging in the hot water, the light, the pristine white sink. All of these are luxuries to me. Then I return to the living room, sit on the sofa, pull out my phone, and play the Uri Geller video. With my other hand, I remove the spoon from around my neck. Uri Geller and I are sort of like friends now. It makes no difference that he has no idea who I am, or that I have no idea if he's still alive. I know the expressions of his smooth and handsome face, his full hair. More than anything, I know his slender fingers, and the way they run over the spoon, tenderly stroking the metal that bends right before the camera.

A few minutes later, I turn off the video and wrap my left hand around the spoon, because the right one still hurts from punching the Georgian. I close my eyes and plead with it: "Just once, just tonight, just one damn time, bend for me." I sit there, whispering my plea. I've got nothing to lose, only to gain. I ask the spoon to let me gain, but it's stubborn, remaining in its normal state. Dog sits beside me on the sofa. I hear Doris snoring in the other room, and it makes me laugh, because she snores as loudly as Noam from my military team, and suddenly I miss all of them so badly.

CHAPTER SIXTEEN

I wake up on the sofa in Doris's apartment. Dog is asleep by my side. The apartment is dim. I hear the rain and the city, and I need to shoot up. Dog stirs awake and licks my hand. I pet him and get up to pee. A surprised man with a smooth face and shorn hair looks back at me from the mirror. I look so different. I feel different, too.

On the dining table, Doris has left a note written in blue pen and small, neat, round handwriting. She also left me some toast. I make myself a cup of coffee, and Dog follows me around like a little kid, someone who needs me. Occasionally I rub his head, which makes him happy. Doris has washed and even dried my clothes, which are now neatly folded on the back of the sofa. I hold them to my face and inhale their fragrance, then pull off Doris's clothes and put on my own.

She trusted me enough to let me stay in her apartment, just left me a key and went off to work. I'm moved by the faith she has in me. Her desire to help comes from genuine, humane warmth. She is a person who actually cares.

I shoot up, then lie down on the sofa, zoning out for a few minutes. Once the high abates a little, though I feel the urge to sit up and practice with the spoon, I decide to skip it this morning. Instead, I make myself another cup of coffee, enjoying the sweetness of the sugar, and a longing awakens in me again, just like the previous night, except this time it's for my family—my mother, my brother, and my sister. I feel the need to cry, so I open my mouth and try to make sobbing sounds, but all that comes out is a contorted bellow, like a wounded animal.

When the rain stops, I start feeling stifled in the apartment. I've become so accustomed to the open air. I decide to take Dog for a walk. He wags his tail, scampering around like a puppy.

I want to get clean. Maybe I can get a job as a counselor for endangered youth, or the guy who goes from school to school, warning kids about the dangers of drugs. Maybe I can give talks professionally, telling my personal story about how a Commando officer ends up as a junkie. I need to get a hold of my liaison officer, to resolve this desertion issue, and have her refer me to a military psychiatrist. The military has to take responsibility, and I need to talk to someone. I need to seek help. I watched my soldiers burning alive in the APC, I took two bullets, I rescued Yehoram's body and received a badge of honor for it. I deserve help. They can't just ignore me.

The sun peeks from between the clouds in a game of light and shadow, wondrous beams of glowing towers birthing a nearly mystical vision. Dog is delighted. He pulls on the leash as if all of this is new to him. He sniffs the air, the curb, the electric poles. He pees on everything in sight and even sneaks into a backyard to take a shit. I pick up after him with pride, throwing out his excrement just like a normal citizen.

In the note Doris had asked me to wait for her. She said it was fine if I decided to leave afterwards, but asked that I at least wait for her to come home after work. "Your clothes are on the sofa. There's some money on the shoe rack near the door. Go get yourself some coffee and enjoy the day."

I think about calling my mother. I don't want to give her false hope, but I feel optimistic. She would be overjoyed to hear from me after spending so long fretting over me, searching the streets for me in all hours of the day and night.

I go to Ovad's. Even though I look different and feel different, as soon as I walk inside the junkie they all know takes over, and I'm not sure whether I should sit down and have coffee like a normal person or ask one of the girls to give me the usual. I get a hold of myself and sit down at a table, Dog by my side. Ovad walks over with coffee in a to-go cup—my ransom.

"Look how handsome you are, Geller! I barely recognized you," he says as he hands over the cup.

"Today I'd like to stay and sit and pay for my drink," I tell him.

"It's an honor, Geller," he smiles. "You look like a completely different person."

"I feel like a completely different person," I reply, trying to smile. It's no longer a natural gesture for me. It feels awkward on my facial muscles, like a twist and a back handspring all at once. "I want my coffee in a mug and I'd like a chocolate croissant too, please." I try to lean into this normalcy.

"Sure thing, Geller, but let me treat you."

"I told you, Ovad, I'm paying today," I fume, then realize this anger belongs to the old Geller, and apologize.

"Don't worry about it. And you're right. One latte in a mug and one chocolate croissant, coming right up."

I'm sweating, feeling out of place, looking around to check if anyone is staring. Then I pick up a newspaper from a nearby table and open it, as if to read. I roll a cigarette and rub Dog's head, and each of these actions makes me feel like an actor pretending to be someone he no longer is.

"One last thing, Ovad," I say when he sets the coffee and the croissant down on the table. "Could you let me make a phone call? I want to talk to my mother."

"Sweetheart, if it's to call your mother I'll *buy* you an iPhone," Ovad says. It warms my heart. He leaves his phone on the table, and I realize I have so many things I didn't have before. I have a latte in a mug and a chocolate croissant and a little money to pay for them, and I have a phone and a newspaper and clean clothes, and in my pocket I have a note from Doris who wants me to stay with her. Maybe I deserve these things after all.

I pick up the phone and dial my mother's number. The ringing matches the beat of my heart. I want so badly to hug her, to tell her I love her, to tell her how I feel, and about Doris and Dog, and that I'm sitting at a café with a newspaper and a coffee and a croissant, and that I think maybe it's time to make a change. I want to tell her that this morning, for the first time, reality seems like a hardened, ugly, itchy crust that I want to peel off, even though the wound of my life underneath will bleed and ache. I'm ready for it. I want to say all these things, but when she picks up, the words lodge in my throat like a paratrooper on a jet in the middle of the sky, looking down, afraid to jump.

"Who's this?" she asks. Her words pull me in, but I remain silent. Then she says my name. I haven't heard anybody speak it in so long. She calls to me, she knows it's me, but I still can't say a word. I want to tell her about my friends who blew up in the APC, and how I can't get the stench of their burning limbs out of my nose. How, while other people smell freshly mowed grass, rain, perfume, and shampoo, I smell corpses and molten steel, how I can't have steak anymore because it feels like I'm eating the scorched flesh of my friends. And I want to tell her about Yehoram, and the moment he got the bullet in his head and his brain spilled over my uniform, and how I was scared to die as I ran down the alleys with him, hearing bullets whizzing by, perforating the walls of buildings, until finally I felt that first bullet hitting me in the thigh and thought it was all over, and all I could think about was the grenade I had in my vest, because I mustn't be captured alive and taken hostage, and my breathing was fast and heavy and the night cooled down as the blood drained out of me, but I just kept running with Yehoram over my shoulder.

Then the second bullet penetrated my shoulder like a hard slap, almost knocking me over, but I managed to straighten up and knew it was a bullet because others kept flying all around me and

I thought that maybe I should have left Yehoram behind, because he was no longer Yehoram, and if I'd left him perhaps I'd have a better chance of surviving.

Again I hear Mom's voice. She's begging me to talk to her, but now my head is back in Gaza, in the field hospital. I lay on a gurney and found a small bit of bone smeared with Yehoram's brains inside my shirt pocket. I didn't know what to do with it, whether I should give it to someone or bury it in the ground or just toss it in the sand. There were lots of soldiers around, as well as Elad, the unit doctor. And I heard them call in a medevac, and knew my guys were about to make the entire neighborhood shake, killing anything in sight, just like the previous day, when we killed a ton of them to redeem our dead, and they were probably all civilians because the terrorists knew better and ran away. They crawled into their burrows like fucking moles, and the only people who remained above were civilians, who had to suffer the bombs that shattered their homes and ripped their organs and blasted their bodies. And poor Dog that Yuval shot in the head, a Hamas Dog who did nothing wrong, just wanted some food or water or attention, and Yuval put a bullet in his head, then smiled like an idiot, and I wanted so badly to punish him, but I couldn't, because what's one dead dog in all this hell?

"Come home, son. Come to Mommy. I love you so much," she says. Her voice is like the voice of the sirens that pulled in the sailors. And I want to go to her, I want to talk, but my throat is blocked. I swallow and try to say just a single word, just "Mom," but nothing comes out.

"Please," she begs.

I can't bear to hear her voice anymore. Before I fall apart, I hang up.

The coffee is still hot, and a large gulp pushes the tears down my throat. I roll myself a cigarette, eat the croissant, give Ovad back his phone, pay for my order—he insists on only charging me for the coffee.

Dog gets up, ready to go, and I think about the heroin I still have. I fight off the feeling. I have to be brave—go to the apartment and wait for Doris there, get in a warm bath and wait for the nausea and the vomiting, the aching muscles and runny nose, the waves of cold and the goosebumps and the teary eyes and the anxiety and the depression. Maybe, with Doris's help, I can kick withdrawal's ass. Symptoms will begin about eight hours after my last hit.

Then I decide I haven't taken my last hit yet. I still have a few left, and it won't be the end of the world if I throw myself a goodbye party. I consider dropping Dog off at home first, but my body decides that it would be just fine if Dog came with me to the dump for an hour or two.

CHAPTER SEVENTEEN

The dump is uglier and smellier than I'd remembered. I feel my way among the piles of debris, and Dog sniffs his own way behind me. How could one night at Doris's apartment make me forget about all this filth? I don't feel like I belong here anymore, but my body still wants to sit in the tattered chair, to wrap the tourniquet around my arm, and shoot up.

I remove Dog's leash and ask him to stay nearby, and he jumps up on the chair and nudges me to make him some room. My heart soars.

I pull four hits from my jacket stash. That's all I have left. Four tiny baggies and I'm done with heroine. One will be enough to start, just to put my mind in order.

The room flickers with light and shadow play, and I'm glad no one else is around. I need some quiet. Thank goodness the Georgian isn't here. I'm not afraid of him, only of my own anger. It's better for both of us that he isn't around. As badly as my hand hurts, his face must hurt worse.

The room smells like shit, like mold, like sweat and feet and rotting carcasses. Yesterday it didn't bother me. I consider getting out of there. Maybe I'd be better off shooting up in a public bathroom. But the heroin has other ideas, and it commands me to stay put. I tighten the tourniquet around my left arm, pick up the empty can and sprinkle it with some water from a bottle by the chair, then empty the white powder into the water. Filter, syringe, orange flame. My body is starved. I press down on the syringe and inject the heroin into my arm, my bloodstream, my brain. I close my eyes and let out a sigh, a greeting.

Dog shoves his nose under my hand. He wants to be petted, wants love. Don't we all? I undo the tourniquet, and remember to sanitize the injection site in spite of my buzz.

They'll start haunting me soon—the tourniquet and the syringe and the heroin. They won't let me leave that easily. I remember how I used to improvise bongs out of glass pipes and different types of plastic bottles, as if rigging military gear. I enjoyed the ritual as much as the smoking itself. I would grind buds and mix them with tobacco, creating a hazy, fragrant concoction. I neglected responsibilities, didn't clean the apartment, lost myself in this new world, tethered to the old world by nothing more than my own self. The wind took care of the rest—scattering everything else—my friends, my parents, my siblings. It scattered my old job and my motorcycle and everything I've ever dreamed of being. The nightmares stopped, and I was too stoned to be in any kind of mood, living in an endless purgatory leading nowhere.

From time to time, Doron would come over, sometimes bringing Ido or Daud with him, and we'd have a proper hang. They'd pass joints around, and I would use the bong because the joints no longer did anything for me. Sometimes they'd talk about the army, and I'd slip in my earbuds and listen to *Classical Mushroom*. The combination of classical music and psychedelic trance allowed me to get stoned without the dead of Shejaiya hovering.

It wasn't bad at all, until the day Yuval came back from South America. I had no idea he'd be coming over with the other guys, but I guess watching his team commander high off his ass was an experience he was not prepared to miss. Anyway, he stood there in the dark stairwell, shooting me that smile of his, the one I used to think was charming but later, in Gaza, discovered it came from his brainstem, the most primordial part that contained his animal essence. It was the same smile he had when he returned the Glock to its leather holster after shooting Dog in the head. I hated that smile and I hated him, and yet he still walked into my apartment with Doron and Ido, and we sat together in my filth on a mattress and pillows I brought into the living room because I no longer needed them in bed.

They rolled joints and I took hits off my bong, and my brain was full of fog and my body was relaxed. Yuval told us about South America, and I heard the words that came out of his mouth but couldn't understand a single thing. I stuffed the bong, lit it up, and watched the sparks fly as the weed burned up into smoke that made its way into my lungs. A big, buzzy wave crashed over me, shooting me up into the sky. The small living room was smoky and dark, because my electricity had been cut off due to unpaid bills. A few candles burned, and I watched my guys, my subordinates, my soldiers who were prepared to charge and die at my command. They were sitting in a semicircle around the candles and the bong and the empty bags of chips and Japanese-style peanuts because Ido is crazy about those. There were also a few bottles of warm Coke—the fridge no longer worked.

I picked up the bong and stuffed it again with another mixture that went up in flames. The candles seemed to merge into a small bonfire that mesmerized me. Doron asked if I was all right, but I couldn't speak. My eyes were fixed on Yuval's smile, and his head, which was turning into Dog's head. He reminded me of the Egyptian dog-God Anubis. I wasn't scared. I was curious. I knew it was just the drugs twisting my perception of reality, and I felt Doron's hand—I know his touch, the weight of his rough hand— on my shoulder. He became my signal operator after Yehoram was killed. When I returned from the hospital, he ran after me like a rat after the Pied Piper. Everyone ran and I ran too, to wherever my own piper pointed me, and he did what his piper told him, and so on and so forth, up to the highest echelon, which ran after the Pied Politician. So I recognized Doron's hand as he grabbed my shoulder. I looked up to him and realized he'd become Anubis too. He had a dog head. They all did.

Yuval slipped the joint between large canine jaws with sharp, drooling fangs and a fat, wet, spongey tongue. Above his mouth was a long, black, damp snout. His smile was that same condescending, scheming smile, and I saw him reaching for his gun. He smiled and smoked and pulled out his gun, wanting to shoot me or Ido or Doron or maybe himself, just like he'd done in Gaza.

And that's when I went mad. I don't remember exactly what I did, but there was yelling and hitting and people holding me down, and the fear was back, all the fear and sorrow and memories and horror, and the drugs didn't help anymore. I started crying over Yehoram and the other dead soldiers and those damn Arabs we were forced to kill when we flattened their homes with D9s and blew them up with missiles and ruined their messed-up lives. And most of all I cried for Dog. I remembered his eyes, a deep black surrounded by yellowish brown. They were the kindest eyes I'd ever seen. They contained a watery glitter, and innocence, and all they wanted was some help, something to eat or drink, or just comfort, because that place was scary. I also wanted comfort, we all did. We were scared but embarrassed, and instead of helping him, instead of petting him and rubbing his belly and scratching behind his ears, Yuval cocked his Glock and shot him in the head, that son of a bitch, and then kicked him too, as if a bullet to the head wasn't enough.

═══════

Dog seems to be asleep now. His eyes are closed and I think I hear him snoring. His fur is nice, his body heat is nice. I pet him and he lifts his head. I guess dogs aren't deep sleepers. He pricks up his ears and looks at me. I think he's asking me to take him back to Doris.

"In a few minutes, Dog. I promise." I keep petting him.

A few days later, I remember asking Doron to hook me up with his dealer. I said I wanted to get some weed. He came to pick me up in his black Golf and we went to the Yemeni Vineyard neighborhood. We parked the car and walked a while, because Doron was convinced the police was tracking Yahya's building. We climbed up the crumbling steps, and when we were outside the door, Doron dialed a number on his phone and the door opened, and I saw a skinny Yemeni man who was the epitome of the word 'junkie.'

"What's going on?" Yahya said, but the question was so limp it barely had the right to exist. It contained no curiosity about what was going on. It wasn't even a question of courtesy. It remained hanging in the air as Yahya went into one of the rooms and Doron hurried after him, and so did I. When we reached the bedroom, we found him lying in a single bed, the window open. It was hot. The whole thing looked like a scene from a film by Almodovar, and I was convinced that detectives would storm the place at any moment, but they didn't, at least not that time.

Doron and Yahya discussed the weed and the price and me. I wasn't really listening, but I got the gist of it. When Doron asked me how much I wanted, I told them I didn't want weed. I was looking for something stronger. Doron laughed, but not because it was funny. He reminded me we were only there to get a little weed, but I told him to shut up because I wanted something stronger.

Yahya didn't seem to care much. He just asked Doron if I could be trusted, and Doron looked at him, then at me, and nodded and said I used to be his commander, that we were like brothers, that we'd fought together in Gaza, and that he had nothing to worry about.

Then Yahya looked at me, as if to make sure I was serious. He no longer waited for me to tell him how much. He just pulled a few baggies of white powder from under his bed and placed two of them in my hand. "I'm giving you one on the house," he said. "It isn't what you think. I'm not doing it to get you hooked so that you buy more. That's going to happen anyway," he laughed and coughed in a sickly combination. "One is on the house for all those fucking Arabs you killed in Gaza." He made a gun shape with his skinny hand and shot me with his pointer finger, then told me the price and lay back down, as if these actions had emptied him of whatever energy he still had left.

Dog hears the sound before I do. He turns his head sharply and barks, and I wonder if I should turn around. It might be the Georgian, and after the way I punched him yesterday, I have no idea what he might do. It could be the police. They've dropped by from time to time, looking for illegal immigrants or just picking on us, because junkies are a great way to kill time on a shift. Anyway, I can sense that Dog wants to get up, so I hold him tightly against my body and whisper to him to relax, everything is fine, I'm here.

"Geller? Are you there?" I haven't seen Crutchy Zvi since that day he scared Doris.

"I'm right here, Zvi."

"Good. I'm glad it's you and not him."

Now I recognize his familiar shuffle. He's got a way of stepping in the mess, shifting things around with his crutches like a large insect moving his antenna around. He finds his corner and sits down.

I turn the chair toward him but can't see him properly. I turn on the flashlight.

"You look good, Geller. A shave and a haircut. Just like a groom on his wedding day!"

"I just had the opportunity, so I took it."

"Next thing you'll tell me you're going into rehab." His tone is disappointed. "Is it that girl, Geller? I could tell right away she felt a special connection with you. Anyone who isn't afraid to come looking for you here must be acting from the heart." He bangs his chest.

He's no idiot, Crutchy Zvi. He's tried to get clean a few times himself. He must understand the logic behind my haircut—if anything was more important to me than shooting up or scoring money for more good drugs, that's saying something.

"Maybe," I say.

"I knew it!" Crutchy Zvi cries out as if he's just won the lottery. "This isn't simple, Geller. I've already told you, it isn't simple. But no one could be happier than me for you and that girl. If you keep doing drugs, you're done for. There's no future here. You've got to succeed, Geller." He lights himself a cigarette. "So how is this going to go? Did your family book you someplace? You can't do it on your own, it's impossible. You start out motivated, and as soon as the sickness begins, everything goes to hell. You need structure. Without supportive structure or medical supervision, without psychological work, it's a no-go, Geller. Just a waste of time."

I think about Doris. I know she can help me. She isn't someone who gives up so easily. I know Doris is all the support I need, but I don't tell him that. I pull out my tobacco and roll myself a cigarette.

"Say, Geller, if you're going into rehab, any chance you can give me some junk?" He feigns nonchalance, but I'm not at all surprised. He's a player, Crutchy Zvi. He knows how to read situations and harness them in his favor. I take a drag from my cigarette. My instinct is to shut him up, tell him to mind his own business and stay away from my junk. But then I remember—I do want to get clean. And getting clean isn't taking time off, it's stopping for good, getting that shit out of my life. "You know what, Zvi? We can have a little party, just you and me. We'll get good and high."

Even though the room is dark, I can see Zvi's toothless mouth stretching into a joyous grin.

CHAPTER EIGHTEEN

I startle awake. Bright light burns my eyes, and words I can't understand are shouted into my ears. There's a stir, bodies moving through the dump, bodies in pressed uniforms, carrying oiled weapons and radios. I smell blood.

"Hold still!" somebody yells at me. This time the words are clear, authoritative, it's someone accustomed to giving orders. If this is the police, I'm better off doing as they say. I might get off easy.

I don't feel too good. My heart is racing. So much blood—that awful, sickening, sweet, metallic smell. The air is almost sticky with warm blood. I'm not sure of anything anymore. Could I be in Gaza?

"His clothes are covered in blood."

"Check out this enormous puddle over here."

"Don't touch anything until forensics gets here, got it? I don't want a contaminated crime scene."

"Get Katzav down here, quick."

Flashes of light in my eyes. The room is painted white, and I spot a few people standing around, as well as Crutchy Zvi in the corner across from me, his head drooped over his chest.

"God, it's like *Silence of the Lambs*."

"I've got to get out of here, I can hardly breathe."

"Why do we have plainclothesmen walking around? Anyone who doesn't have to be here, get out!"

Sirens wail outside. My body is burning up and I'm trembling. *I'm not in Gaza, I'm not in Gaza, I'm not in Gaza.* I repeat the mantra, trying to convince my brain that this isn't war. I don't know what's going on, but it isn't war. I'm in the dump, and so is Crutchy Zvi. I'm still sitting in the chair after we partied like mad. We may have even overdone it. I hope that idiot didn't OD, that's all I need, him dead of an overdose. The blood between my fingers is viscous, unmistakable. Anyone who's held a handful of blood once can never forget the feeling. I haven't forgotten. There was blood like this in Gaza. But before I dissociate, I remember Dog and I remember Doris.

"I need Dog! Where's Dog?" I ask, disoriented.

"Shut your damn mouth!" someone yells and slaps me. The slap doesn't hurt, but it's like a punch to the heart. I can't see a thing in this festival of flashlights and I decide to shut up so that they can have no complaints, no excuses to beat me up.

They lift me violently off the chair, twist my arms behind my back, and bind me with handcuffs that squeeze my wrists, then half-lead half-drag me outside. They push me, hard, and one of them tells me I'm under arrest. He doesn't say "abducted" and doesn't have an Arabic accent. He's speaking Hebrew. My brain is searching for clues to tell me whether I'm here or there. My feet falter and I nearly fall. They hold me up. I can't breathe, my breath catches in the dense space between my stomach and my back. I have no air, I fight for every breath, and I'm about to pass out. Flickering lights blind my eyes, blue and red and as loud as voiceless screams. They invade my brain, flood my pupils. I hear radios, people talking, and I can't breathe, I have no air. I dive into the abyss, praying somebody rescues me. I look up to search for a chopper, but all I see is darkness and buildings and I'm in Tel Aviv, not Gaza, not Gaza, not Gaza.

Please, God. I fall to my knees and someone kicks my back, hard. It loosens my breath but knocks me on my face. My hands are still cuffed behind my back, and I think my nose is broken because I hear bones cracking, like a dry branch snapping, and I feel blood streaming from my nose and drenching my undershirt. I'm barefoot. I remember telling my soldiers it's better to be killed than taken hostage. If there is a hostage swap, our government will be willing to give up a thousand of their terrorists for each one of our soldiers, and we mustn't give them a thousand. It's better to die than be taken hostage. And now they're taking me hostage.

They grab my shirt from behind and pick me up as if I'm a little boy. I throw up. I hear the people around me cursing, and I puke blood and the chocolate croissant and as I empty my stomach I empty my soul. Then I take another slap to the face, and this time sparks fly from my nose straight into my brain, but I don't care, let them do whatever they want with me, let them beat me, torture me. I'm not a Golani officer anymore. I'm a doormat. *They kidnapped a doormat,* I tell myself and burst out laughing, because the Hamas terrorists wanted to abduct an officer but got a doormat instead.

"You think this is funny?" someone asks.

Where are the goddamned choppers? I guess I say it out loud because one of these guys asks me what I'm talking about. I don't answer, I don't intend to tell them anything apart from my personal identification number. They can kill me just like they did Yehoram. I'm drenched in sweat and I'm shivering and I'm covered with blood and my nose is broken and I have no idea what happened. The Hamas guys are dressed like police officers, Gaza looks like Tel Aviv, and I've lost Dog, and Doris will be sad, and what happened to Crutchy Zvi? He must have overdosed. Damn, how I could use a hit right now. I want to die, I want that bastard God to take me, I want those sons of bitches to shoot me in the head, to spill my brain, to dead check me again and again, until it's clear to everyone that I won't be getting up again. I'm happy to die. But then I think of my mother, and again I'm filled with fear. *Just don't let anyone tell her I'm dead. Not after what happened to Dad. She won't be able to take it.* I saw what happened to the parents of soldiers who were killed. They went out like candles. Their sons' deaths extinguished their hearts, just like a flame goes out with the squeeze of a finger and a thumb.

I almost don't notice them shoving me into the car. I think it's a squad car. What's the Israeli police doing in Shejaiya? Maybe I'm not in Gaza? Maybe I've already been rescued in some sophisticated operation? Maybe Uri Geller told them where Hamas was holding me and now they won't have to release a thousand terrorists in exchange for me? Maybe my team rescued me? I hope none of them was killed because of me. The car is moving and I'm inside of it. I think they're taking me to meet the Prime Minister. They'll probably have a press conference. I wish Doris was here, I wish Dog was here, and Amir and Daphne and Mom. I wish Dad was here.

The drive is short. The car pulls up and someone drags me out. The cuffs squeeze my wrists. My breathing is calmer now. I think the attack is over. Gaza is gone. They're taking me to the police precinct. I climb the stairs. My nose hurts but is no longer bleeding. A uniformed officer is holding my hand, dragging me as if I were a little boy delivered to the principal's office. There are hallways and doors and rooms like a goddamn maze. He's tall, this police officer, and his body is strong and muscular. He reminds me a little of the way I used to be. There's a Duvdevan military pin on his uniform. So he served in Duvdevan and now he's a cop. I'm familiar with the pin because I met Duvdevan fighters when I was in officer training, and later in all sorts of operations in the West Bank. Great fighters, those Duvdevan guys.

"Sit down," he says, pushing me onto a chair in a small interrogation room.

"My hands hurt," I say.

"I can't touch your handcuffs. Patience. Katzav will be here soon, he'll decide what to do with you."

"What to do with me?" I repeat. "What to do with me?!" I suddenly scream.

"Katzav will be here soon," the ex-Duvdevan cop says and leaves.

I'm at a police station, I'm almost certain of that. I have no idea what time it is or what day it is, but I know I messed up big time with Dog and Doris is going to kill me. I promised to wait for her until she gets home from work, but instead I went to shoot up with Crutchy Zvi. I've been arrested a few times, but they've never made such a big deal of it before. The cuffs hurt my wrists and my nose is pounding. That fucking Katzav will be here soon, and that's the first thing I want him to do—loosen these handcuffs a little. But until he gets here, I have enough time to consider my life and what's become of it. I know it isn't too late. I know I can still find my way out of this. Doris can help me. We can live together and take care of Dog. I'm dying for a hit, my body is sweating its demands. I shiver, my stomach hurts. The handcuffs are the least of my troubles. I need a hit and the cop knows it. Now I'll have to wait and see how long they'll decide to torture me for. They know I need a hit and they've tied my hands as if I've murdered somebody. As if I'm some criminal.

The door opens and a man walks in—Katzav or somebody else. He also looks like someone who served in an elite unit. I've met a ton of guys from Commando units, but no one is as tough as Golani guys. He's holding a disposable cup fragrant with steaming black coffee. I used to love black coffee. Now I prefer a latte with four or five sugars.

He closes the door behind him, sets his cup on the table, and sits down across from me. He's wearing a tight black shirt that shows off his muscles. He has short hair and the handsome face of a movie star—symmetrical, smooth skin, twinkling eyes. He looks at me for a long time, and I wait for him to say what he has to say, what I've heard dozens of times before from all sorts of cops who've arrested or detained me. That there's a wave of burglaries in the area, that some old ladies had their purses snatched, that mothers are scared for their children. As if, being a junkie, I must also be a pedophile or a kidnapper. I wait for him to spew that usual shit and release me back to the dump, because I'm dying for a hit.

"I need your name, your I.D. number, and I need you to tell me exactly what happened there." Katzav's eyes pierce me.

"Man, I need a hit," I tell him. I know it's a game. I know he wants to torture me, otherwise he would have let me go already. There may truly be a junkie upsetting the neighborhood. They may truly be conducting an investigation. But not at my expense. I barely ever steal, and you could count on one hand the number of times I've stolen something with the intent of scoring a hit. I'm a junkie of good stock—well educated, a Commando officer. I sit outside of Ovad's café and beg for change. It's a game now, but my body's in no mood for games. "Let me out of these handcuffs and give me a hit, and then I'll tell you anything you want to know."

This Katzav guy stares at me, like he wants me to try to decipher his expression, but I could care less. I'm not even thinking about him. I don't feel well.

"What do I look like?" he asks. "A drug dealer?"

"You look like a son of a bitch," I say without thinking. This guy is getting on my nerves.

But he doesn't get upset. He just takes a long sip of his coffee, sets the cup down on the table, picks up his phone, glances at it, then looks back at me with a half-smile, so that I can tell I'm not even worth beating up. If anyone else called him a son of a bitch, he would break his face. But not me—I'm not even worth a slap. "Let's start at the beginning, okay? If you cooperate, I promise I'll get you some methadone," he finally says.

"I don't need methadone. I need a hit!" I scream.

He picks up his coffee again, holding it between his hands as if to keep warm, then leans back comfortably in his chair. He's got time, he's in no rush. He's here on the clock and he knows I don't have that kind of time. With every passing moment, my body becomes sicker and more anxious.

He takes another long sip of his coffee, the liquid making a whistling sound as it passes between his lips. We look at each other for a few long seconds before he pulls out a pack of cigarettes and lights one. I look at him and try to maintain my restraint, trying not to show him that I could easily bite his face off, that I'm this close to banging my head against the table.

"If you want the methadone, you've got to start talking," he says, taking a long puff from his cigarette. "You don't have to say anything, you can wait for a lawyer, you can sit here and do nothing. Makes no difference to me, we've got everything we need."

I don't understand what he's trying to do, I don't understand what he wants from me, why he doesn't do what he needs to do and then put me in the squad car to drop me off in the hellhole where they found me. That's what they do best. They never actually try to help, just to pretend to be working. They pick up a junkie, kick him around for a while, then return him to his lair.

"What do you want from me?" I ask.

"Say, have you seen yourself lately?" he asks, smiling. "I want you to tell me everything from the beginning."

I look myself over. In the light of the interrogation room, I realize I'm covered in blood, I stink of it, I'm drenched like a butcher in a slaughterhouse. My undershirt is drenched and my military pants are stained and my hands are red and sticky. "You broke my nose, now I'm covered in blood," I say.

That must be funny, because now he isn't just smiling, he's actually laughing. The cigarette smokes itself between his fingers while his coffee cools on the table. He's laughing as if I just told a joke.

"What do you want to hear?" I ask, because I don't know what he wants me to tell him. Then I think maybe this is about the fentanyl I stole from the hospital. Maybe they caught me on a security camera, or maybe Crutchy Zvi or the Georgian told an intelligence officer I stole it. Junkies aren't exactly trustworthy. Yes, it must be the fentanyl. I feel bad about Dog and think about how pissed off Doris must be. They could definitely screw me over for theft. If they want to, they could screw me over, hard.

"Is it the fentanyl?" I ask.

"Fentanyl?"

From the look in his eyes I realize he has no idea what I'm talking about, so I shut up.

"Can you tell me what I'm being detained for?" I ask in my calmest voice.

He laughs again. "No problem, we'll play this your way. Someone will come in to take your fingerprints soon. They'll check your clothes, take pictures. If you don't want to talk, that's fine by me. This case is closed."

"I don't know what you're talking about," I tell him.

"Of course you don't. But you'll remember. I promise, you'll remember everything," he says. Then he gets up and leaves the room.

CHAPTER NINETEEN

The most painful thing was that they took the spoon from me. More than the beating, more than the handcuffs, more than the broken nose. They stripped me and took my clothes away. They took my pictures and my fingerprints. They asked for a DNA sample and didn't wait for my approval. They did all of these things rudely and aggressively, but the most painful thing was that they took the Uri Geller spoon from me, stripping me of the only hope my soul had of redemption. Now I have no spoon and no hope, and my body hurts, my body is sick, it needs the medicine they won't give me. If they detained a diabetic, they'd give him some insulin. If they detained someone with high blood pressure, they'd give them beta blockers. But they won't give me my medication because in their eyes I'm not sick. Instead they drag me back to the interrogation room, where that Katzav cop sits waiting as if he never even left the room, wearing that black shirt that shows off his toned muscles, the cigarette he seems to have never finished smoking burning between his fingers. "Welcome back," he says, signals for me to sit, then tells the officer escorting me to leave the room and close the door behind him. "I already know who you are, but I'm not about to tell you what I know, because, unlike you, I've got time. I'm not jonesing for a hit or waiting for methadone. You, on the other hand, are just launching off. I know what you're going through. I've witnessed it dozens of times. Your agony hasn't started yet, but it's coming, it's on the way, you'll be screaming for that methadone. I'm waiting to hear the whole story, from start to finish. If your story satisfies me, you'll get what you need."

I don't listen to him. I no longer care. He doesn't exist. None of this exists. Not Katzav the interrogator, not the chair, not the room, not the precinct. I drown into the pain that emerges from my body like sounds floating out of a music box. I'm cold and shivering, my joints hurting as if someone just smashed a hammer against them, my nose is dripping, my eyes are tearing, my stomach is turning. I can't calculate how many hours have gone by since my latest hit, but it must be long enough for my body to start screaming.

"I need to throw up," I say.

He says nothing, just pulls out the trashcan from under his table and passes it to me. But I throw up on the floor before the trashcan reaches me. I mostly vomit liquid with some unidentified lumps floating around in it.

Katzav gets up and leaves. I'm so sick I can't even sit up. I trickle to the floor and curl up like a fetus. Now I'm too hot. I'm burning up from the inside. I tear off the long-sleeved undershirt they gave me and try to absorb some cold from the floor. I'm burning up and trembling cold.

I feel someone picking me up. The cuffs are tight, but they're like mosquito bites compared to the pain assaulting my nerves. A pain that is a way of being. I have trouble isolating it, all of me inside of it as if inside a bubble, head and stomach and legs and hands and scalp. I'm a hunk of aching flesh.

They take me into another office, and I'm sitting across from Katzav again, and he smiles at me pleasantly.

"Golani officer, badge of honor. Who would have thunk it? What happened to you, man? Look at yourself?" He clicks his tongue. "It'll be a great help to you if you tell me everything. It'll cleanse your soul. As a bonus, I'll make sure they take into account that you're a hero soldier. You just have to tell me exactly what happened there. I don't want to jump to conclusions, because reality is usually more complicated. I know that things sometimes snowball, and you can find yourself with blood on your hands without meaning to."

I have trouble following what he's saying. I feel as if I'm about to die.

"Want a cigarette?"

I nod, and he lights a cigarette and places it between the fingers of my cuffed hand. I barely smoke. I inhale and cough my lungs out, my stomach turning. I need to throw up again.

"Tell me what happened there," he says, and I don't understand what he wants from me. All of a sudden, all the thoughts that I tried to push away with all the weed and then all the heroin come up, and I feel that fear again, the same fear I felt when everything blew up, when my subordinates and friends exploded in front of my eyes, and redheaded Yehoram, how he died in my arms. It's all too much, I start crying and the tears shower my face. I feel Yehoram's blood dripping down my face in an irritatingly monotonous trickle, burning my cheeks, streaming in narrow rivers of fire and burning my neck and chest, and I beg the interrogator for methadone, I'm dying.

"Don't worry, you won't die. I've seen my fair share of junkies jonesing."

"But Yehoram's blood… it's burning my body," I say.

"Was that his name? Yehoram?"

"Yes, Yehoram," I say, rubbing my back against the seatback because Yehoram's blood is now burning me there. It leaves a trail of itchiness behind it, like tiny ants pinching my skin.

"So you killed him?" he asked.

"You could say I bear some responsibility," I say, then ask for the trashcan and this time I manage to keep the content of my stomach down before the can is in my hands. "Give me a little methadone, please," I finally manage.

"Just a few more questions." Katzav is jotting things down, and

I can't really follow what's happening because the cigarette butt is burning my fingers. I flick it into the trashcan full of vomit.

"So you were at that dump. Then what happened? Did he piss you off?"

"The dump? Yes, we took it over and used it as a lookout point before invading the neighborhood," I mumble. My eyes are tearing and my head hurts and I'm scared, I'm so scared. "We were lying in wait—not that there was really any waiting, because everything all around started to explode, and the dump wasn't really a dump before the IDF bombed the shit out of it. It was a house where a Palestinian family used to live. It may have been an innocent family, or maybe some Hamas members lived there. Judging by the toys all over the floor there were definitely a few kids."

Katzav bangs on the table very hard, and it vibrates through the room like a bomb. I jump up and my eyes flicker from Shejaiya to his face. "I need you focused, you can't fall apart on me now," he says, his eyes burning. "You were sitting in the dump, you and Yehoram, and then what? Tell me how it started and what made you do it."

"What made me do it?" I repeat.

"I'm all ears." He lays his hands out on the table.

"What time is it?"

"It's almost noon."

I try to calculate how many hours I've gone without shooting up and how much worse I'm about to feel. "Can I have another cigarette?"

He says nothing, just lights a cigarette, takes a long puff, then passes it to me as if we're sharing a joint.

The smoke I inhale into my faulty lungs causes me to cough again. It moves from the lungs to the stomach, then down to my testicles and all the way to my feet. "I have diarrhea," I say.

He sucks in air like someone about to lose his temper, but then he yells and someone comes in to try and help me up, but when he pulls on my cuffed hands I feel an intense pain, like electricity shooting from my hands to my brain, and I see Dog's face a moment before Yuval shot him in the head, and fear takes over because I'm so confused I have no idea what's going on, and the hand holding me looks like a terrorist's hand, I'm not sure about anything anymore, so I jump up from the chair, head-butt the guy, and try to run away, but hands take hold of me, and from that moment on I get the shit beaten out of me, because this interrogator, whose name I thought was Katzav, but now I'm almost certain he's a Hamas member, he jumps on me, and a few more people immediately join in, all kicking and punching me, and the truth is I can hardly feel it because my body hurts so badly as it is, and now I'm going to be kidnapped into Gaza and will probably be held there in some underground hellhole just like Gilad Shalit, and I'm going to die and never see my mother's face ever again.

CHAPTER TWENTY

Dog walks down the street full of purpose, dragging an orphaned leash behind him. Since the rain has stopped, he can easily track the smells he left behind when he marked his path on poles and walls.

He arrives at Doris's building at first light. He recognizes the place, the stone wall out front, the fragrant myrtle bushes in the yard, the specific blend of aromas that exists nowhere else.

He climbs the stairs as he's done so many times before, needing no light since everything is drenched with the familiar smells. He plops down on the door mat, rubs himself against it with pleasure, twisting around, trying to fill his fur with the odor of home. He pricks his ears: Doris is asleep, snoring loudly. The door is locked.

After some time, he can't restrain himself any longer. He scratches at the door and whines, wanting to come in and find his spot in her bed, in the heat of her body, in the words she tells him and in her comforting caresses. Finally he hears her rising, her heavy footfalls along the floor. He smells her body before she even opens the door, before she turns the key. He wags his tail and barks though he knows it isn't allowed—not in the middle of the night, while everyone is asleep. He knows, but he can't resist the urge. The joy overcomes the prohibition.

Doris is excited to see him. He jumps up and licks her hand. She brings him inside, kneels, takes hold of his neck, removes the leash, and kisses his face. "Where were you, Dog? I was worried sick about you! And where's Geller? Did he leave you all alone? Are you hungry?" She walks over to his bowl and fills it with the Kibble he doesn't love but to which he has grown accustomed. And right now he's hungry, so he starts eating at once. But when Doris walks away to get dressed he follows her, jumping up on her bed and curling up, his eyes tracking her movements.

"Where have you two been, Dog? I'm so worried about Geller," she says, strapping on a bra and slipping on a tank top.

Dog's eyelids droop but he isn't sleeping. He jumps off the bed when Doris walks over to the kitchen and flicks on the electric kettle. Now she'll make herself a cup of coffee and then sit down and smoke a cigarette. Dog is familiar with her early morning routine. He positions himself by the chair where she usually sits, his head at the perfect spot for her to pet him. But Doris pours the coffee in a disposable cup, not a mug. She puts on a wide coat, doesn't linger to slip the leash around Dog's neck, and even though he's just gotten off the street, he joins her as she walks out.

Doris smokes her cigarette outside. It's cold, and the smoke from her cigarette mixes with the steam from her breath. The night is almost over, dawn is stalling, the street is empty of people and cars. In a few minutes, the city will shake off the sleep and the noise will peel off the shell of quiet, but for now they walk as if in another, quieter, emptier, calmer city. In the distance, a siren rips the silence, dragging behind it the crude beeping of a reversing truck, the growling of an engine, and the yelling of bakery owners, and anyway, as the first rays of light strip the darkness, Doris realizes that the moment has passed. A flock of starlings lands on top of the large ficus, making a racket as if it's the middle of the day, announcing loudly that the night is gone and the morning is here, but outside it's still dark and it seems to Doris that the entire day will be winter, and how lovely it would have been to remain under the down blanket, but now that Dog is back, and back without Geller, she has to find him and make sure nothing terrible happened, even though she's certain something has. She knows Geller would not have let Dog loose just like that, pictures him lying in his own vomit in the dump, having overdosed. That dangerous man he called the Georgian scares her too. There's no telling what he might do after Geller punched him. She had to hold herself from going to the dump all of last night. She promised Geller she wouldn't go.

From a distance, she spots the police cruisers spraying their colorful lights on the building walls all around, as if this were a dance club. An ambulance, police officers, and a few locals, some in pajamas and slippers, stand around, watching.

She walks with Dog up to the police barricade. "What happened here?" she asks.

A guy in a red sweatsuit says there was a murder.

"Who was murdered?" she gasps.

"Some homeless guy, it looks like."

She feels her body draining of blood. She takes a few steps, then sits down on the sidewalk.

"You okay?" the guy asks.

Dog comes up to lick her face, returning some warmth to her cold cheeks. She breathes heavily and signals with her hand to the guy that she's fine, but he doesn't seem satisfied.

"Are you sure?" He crouches down to her level.

Dog growls and bares his teeth at him.

"Thanks, but I'm fine," she says.

After the guy walks away, she tells Dog, "You've got to be a little friendlier." She pats his head, then gets up, takes a few deep breaths to steady herself, and returns to the barricade. Two officers stand there, a male officer with white hair and droopy cheeks covered with white stubble, and a female officer with a short, boyish haircut.

"I think I know him."

"Know who?" the male officer asks.

"The homeless man who was murdered." Doris can't believe the words coming out of her mouth.

"How do you know him?"

"I had him over to my place just yesterday, and this is his dog," she says, tears in her eyes.

"There's a lady here who claims she knows the victim," the cop says into his radio. The female officer stands nearby, not comforting Doris, even though she's crying. Instead, the woman stands there with a tough, tired face.

The cop asks Doris to join him and together they approach a man in plainclothes.

"Here she is," the cop tells him.

"Superintendent Daniel Harari, Tel Aviv Homicide Squad," the guy introduces himself and shakes Doris's hand limply. He's shorter than she is, with a small paunch. He doesn't look much like a cop to her, and certainly not like any cop she's seen on TV. "Do you mind taking a look and identifying the body?" he asks.

"You don't look like a Daniel," she says, because it's the first thing that comes to mind.

He laughs, his smile stretching up to his sideburns. Then he leads her toward the ambulance. Lightning fills the skies and Doris's heart, then thunder shakes the world. She drags herself behind the superintendent, calling Dog to follow.

"Wait a minute," she tells two men who are busy loading a stretcher carrying something that used to be human and is now just flesh wrapped in a white bag.

For a moment, Doris can't figure out why she's so sad, as sad as if she's lost a beloved relative. She barely knew Geller. And yet she's shivering, while Superintendent Daniel Harari's hand is steady as a rock, and perhaps just because it rests upon her shoulder is she able to stand there as the bag is unzipped. Then she lets out a yell, feeling the cop's grip tightening.

She doesn't recognize Geller. There's a dead face in the bag, with half-open dead eyes and wild hair and bloodied facial hair, but it isn't Geller, it's a different junkie, much more of a junkie than Geller. Even when he was alive he wasn't really alive. She lets out a big exhale, then bends over, throws down her hands, and runs them through her hair. Dog licks her face, her heart empties of sorrow and fills with hope.

"Are you all right? Is that your guy?"

Strange, but she likes Harari's question. She shakes her head no. "It isn't Geller," she manages as she stands back up and looks into the cop's eyes.

"Who's this Geller guy?" he asks.

"Geller, he lives here in the dump," she says, pointing at what used to be a home. "But this isn't him, this is Crutchy Zvi," she adds, then starts laughing.

The superintendent signals to the ambulance driver that he can load the stretcher, then turns to her again. "You know him, too?"

"Not exactly. I saw him once."

He gives her a long look, and she knows he's wondering how this woman with the dog knows so many junkies. "Come by the station to give a statement, please. In the meantime, I suggest finding shelter from the rain. You're soaking wet." He gives her his business card and leaves.

Doris decides to go home, take a hot shower, and have breakfast. Geller's probably disappeared into some other hole, or maybe he met some friends and decided to shoot up someplace else.

"What are you so pleased with yourself for?" she finds herself annoyed with Dog, who saunters elegantly, ears pricked and tail wagging, busy sniffing around. "Come home already," she tells him. Then she continues to monologue. "Ungrateful, that's what I have to say. I took him into my home, accepted him just as he is. I never asked him for anything. Then he gets up and leaves without a word? Doesn't he care that I'm worried about him? I'm nothing to him. I guess that's how it goes with junkies. Nothing matters to them more than drugs. Come on, Dog, let's go home. It's best if we forget all about him."

CHAPTER TWENTY-ONE

Eventually, they gave me methadone and even let me take a shower, so I'm feeling a little better. I'm sitting in Katzav's interrogation room, across from an interrogator I haven't seen before. He looks like a good guy before he even opens his mouth, and once he does he's practically Elijah the Prophet. He just wants what's best for me, asks me to help him help me. He almost sounds in love. He tells me that the judges are very impressed with defendants who play along, and that sometimes it can even cut a sentence by half. I figure that if Katzav is the bad cop then this guy must be the good cop, so I take advantage of the situation and ask for a can of Coke and a cigarette. He smiles amiably, then speaks into his phone, and a few seconds later someone comes inside with a Coke and a pack of cigarettes. The good cop opens the can and hands it to me along with a cigarette and a lighter, making sure to clarify that now that he's helping me, it's time for me to help him.

The cold Coke settles my stomach. My hand is shaking, but the methadone has done the trick, and the withdrawal symptoms have abated.

He watches me through his friendly-uncle glasses. He has a warm smile and thinning gray hair. He's wearing a plaid flannel lumberjack shirt and has a nervous blinking tic.

"What do you want to know?" I ask, puffing on the cigarette.

"The guys tell me you prefer to be called 'Geller,'" he says, still smiling.

It's true. That's what I prefer, because there's nothing else in me beyond Geller.

"I want to know what happened in the dump. You think you can tell me what happened there, Geller?" he asks sweetly.

"We were sitting there, Crutchy Zvi and I. I had decided to kick off the habit. I even called my mother. I was going to have one last party, and because I had a few hits left, I offered Crutchy Zvi some. I knew if we didn't polish it all off, there was no chance I'd have the will power to throw it out."

Elijah the Prophet jots down everything I tell him, nodding. "And what happened next?"

"Nothing. Nothing happened. We talked a little, laughed, then shot up and each lost ourselves in thoughts. Then we shot up again, and the next thing I remember is all your friends beating the shit out of me."

I look at his flushed cheeks, his eyes narrowing behind the silver glasses, and for a moment I think he's going to bark at me, because his lips tremble. But he manages to maintain his composure, only the pen between his fingers tapping nervously on the table. "So you're saying you can't remember?"

All of a sudden, he looks like an IRS clerk rather than a cop.

I finish the cigarette and put it out in the ashtray, then down what's left in the Coke can and set it on the table. I try hard. I grab my head in my hands and run everything that happened through my mind, trying to come up with anything else, but that's truly all I can remember.

"Listen, you're an IDF officer, you received a badge of honor. You think the judges aren't going to take that into account? Now, I want you to understand: if you start playing along, I'm sure you'll get off easy."

"Could you at least tell me what I'm being accused of?" I say.

He gives me a long look, and I see his lips about to part to speak, and he seems to be fighting it off, until finally he leans back so much I'm afraid his chair will collapse. "We're accusing you of murder, of course."

"Murder? You're accusing me of murder? Who, exactly, did I murder?"

"His name is Zvi Berg, but from what I gather, you know him as Crutchy Zvi."

"Crutchy Zvi was murdered?" My thoughts are bouncing around like balls in a pinball machine. "Maybe he OD'd, or just had a heart attack? Why are you so sure he was murdered?"

"He didn't OD and he didn't have a heart attack. He was murdered viciously, and I want you to consider very carefully whether you may have murdered Zvi Berg without remembering it."

"No chance," I say decisively.

"If you can't remember, how can you be so sure?"

"Because I'm not a murderer!" I yell. But deep down I'm not convinced that's true.

"You don't understand what we have on you."

"Well, come on, then—tell me what you have on me." I'm getting annoyed now. *Good cop my ass.*

"We've got his blood all over your clothes, we've got your fingerprints on the knife, we've got forensic evidence, we've got a closed case. I don't even need you to plead guilty. Your admission is just a bonus, something to open the eight o'clock news with, so that the nice blond anchor can look into the eyes of everybody in Israel and tell them how the celebrated Commando officer who carried his soldier out of Gaza under Hamas fire, confessed to murdering a poor homeless man. That's all, Geller."

The things he says blast through my head like bullets—boom, boom, boom, one after the other. I don't know if he's lying, I don't know if this cop is just playing mind games on me, but I also have no idea if I murdered Crutchy Zvi. My memory is a barren wasteland. We sat in the dump and I invited him to party with me. I had stuff and knew I was getting clean. I knew Doris was my chance to get out of the shit, and when I think of her I realize how badly I fucked this up—I have no idea where Dog is or what's going on with her, and I'm in custody, and how could Crutchy Zvi be dead? How could he have been murdered? I would never, ever, hurt him, ever!

Spent, I tell the cop, "I want to sleep. Please."

"No problem at all, Geller. You get to go to sleep in a minute. I just want you to think carefully and tell me if there's any chance you murdered Zvi Berg. You took drugs, maybe had too much to drink… Maybe it has something to do with what happened to you in Gaza? We've seen this kind of thing before—people suffering from PTSD who suddenly commit a murder."

I think about his words. They sit in my brain, as heavy as lead. Crutchy Zvi had gotten on my nerves more than once. Maybe, with everything that happened in Gaza, I could have killed him? Maybe he drove me crazy, or maybe I believed he was a terrorist and stabbed him or hit him in the head with a brick. I could have easily killed that kid I pulled my gun on, I really don't know anymore. So I start crying, no tears at first because my eyes are dry and itchy and burning, but sorrow can draw water from a rock, and the tears burst forth, and I sit there spraying like a sprinkler. I cry for my friends in Gaza and for what happened to me and my father and my broken family. And I cry for Crutchy Zvi.

"Let it all out, Geller, you'll feel much better," the cop says. I feel his hand resting on my shoulder, like a warrior comforting a friend at the end of a battle. "If there's a chance you murdered him, if there's any such chance, you have to remember, Geller," he insists.

"I don't know!" I scream, because I really don't know.

"I want to hear you say it." He squeezes my shoulder, his fingers digging into my skin, crushing my heart.

"I have to sleep, I can't take this anymore. I need a hit," I mutter.

"Say the words, and I'll let you sleep for as long as you want. Just say the words, and as soon as you wake up I'll set you up with some junk. Say it, and you'll feel much better."

I've killed so many Arabs that one more Crutchy Zvi doesn't matter anymore, and his hand on my shoulder, I can't stand it.

"Say it, Geller. Tell me how you murdered him."

"I can't. I don't remember anything. I don't know what happened there. We were sitting around, shooting heroin, but—"

"And then he did or said something that drove you mad?"

"I can't remember."

"Then remember, and tell me what you did. Tell me and then go to sleep. It's that simple," he says into my ear.

Then I whisper, "It's possible I killed him."

"It isn't just possible, Geller. You killed him. But for now, I think that's enough," he says, his tone calm, content. "Go get a few hours of sleep, and when we wake you up you'll start remembering exactly how you killed him and why. Then we'll take you to the dump and you'll do a reenactment for us."

I feel my eyes fluttering shut. I truly don't care about anything anymore.

CHAPTER TWENTY-TWO

Doris's apartment sinks into a silent sadness, disturbed only by the monotonous rattling of the fridge. She's glad Geller's alive, but that isn't enough to abate the weight of pain crushing her lungs, streaming through her blood vessels, filling her organs. She's feeling lost, as if forgotten in the middle of the ocean, every wave liable to pull her into the abyss, with no one in the world to save her.

Dog doesn't understand why she crawled into bed and burst into tears. She sleeps just a few minutes, then wakes up, calls Rosa, and apologizes meekly, explaining she won't be coming to clean that day. She won't share what's going on even when Rosa insists. Immediately afterwards she falls asleep and wakes up again around noon. It seems the rain has stopped and the sun is shining brightly on the world, which aggravates her. She ignores Dog's excitement as he prances around her, swallows two sleeping pills, and goes back to bed.

The next time she wakes up, the wind whistles between the shutters like lips emitting wintery whistles.

Dog has to relieve himself. He pleads with Doris in every way he knows how to take him for a walk, but she won't budge. The sorrow collapses her, and she's sprawled out on the bed like a boxer that's been knocked out. Her eyes are closed and her soul is flipping through memories of the child who was her entire world, whom she lost in that awful accident. Is he the one she's been looking for in Geller? She's so accustomed to her routine, moving by force of inertia, knowing full well that if she stops to think, there's no knowing what she might do.

Dog licks her hand as it dangles down the side of the bed, a hand bearing the signs of all that hard work. She pulls her hand away, as if to say he must wait, she doesn't have the energy to take him out now.

Eventually she gets out of bed, and Dog can't restrain himself from barking with joy. The floor is cold against her feet, but there's an inner heat burning inside her. The kitchen is empty and dark and she isn't sure what time it is. It might be night or it might be early morning. She goes to pee, then to the kitchen, turns on the kettle, and glances at the clock. She's spent so many hours sleeping. The smell of coffee awakens her, and she pulls on a thin windbreaker, socks and sneakers, grabs a pack of cigarettes and a lighter, and shoves them into her jacket pocket. Dog runs to the door and waits for her, sitting upright. She attaches his leash and takes him out.

They walk along a road mottled with spots of wetness where the asphalt has sunken. Dog is happy. He frolics between the exhales of the wind that has scattered leaves on the ground, and Doris lets him play.

All of a sudden, Dog smells blood. He startles and sniffs the air, his body no longer relaxed. He tracks the scent, pulling Doris behind as she struggles to balance her lit cigarette and lukewarm coffee. "Enough, Dog, stop it, let's go home," she scolds.

But Dog insists and pulls on the leash, determined to follow the scent trail maddening his senses. And perhaps this determination is what convinces her to give in and drag behind him like a somnambulant.

Dog's nose leads him, and he's already so close it's as if the blood is practically in his nostrils. He stops by a large metal container full of construction debris. The smells can no longer mislead him, he can taste the blood on his tongue. He rises on his hind legs, scratching the container with his front paws as if it were the door to his home, barking.

"What did you find there?" she asks Dog, then looks into the container, shifting around some garbage and an old sink, and spots a bag of clothes underneath it.

CHAPTER TWENTY-THREE

"Look, it's important that you understand what they're accusing you of." That's what the attorney appointed by the state says immediately after introducing himself. He looks a little older than I am, but his face is boyish, with brown hair that's been carefully coiffed with the sticky products most often used by teenagers. He wears narrow glasses and reeks of cologne. He pulls a folder from his briefcase and flips through his papers for a few seconds.

Then he tells me he used to be a lieutenant in paratrooper Battalion 890, and that he read about my background. He knows about the badge of honor, knows I fought in Gaza, about the stakeout in Shejaiya and all the casualties in the APC. He also read the story about Yehoram, and how I was wounded while carrying him over my shoulder under fire.

"They have no idea how that kind of thing wounds our souls," he says, patting my back. I feel as if he truly understands me. "Murder is the worst offense in the penal code," he explains, smoothing his suit. I fix my eyes on him. His are blue, as clear as glass. "Voluntary manslaughter is the most critical injury, because it denies man his most basic right—the right to life. I'm explaining these things in the driest terms because I want you to understand that if the judges determine this is murder, and not another kind of crime, such as manslaughter or negligent killing, the sentence will be a life sentence, regardless of the cause."

He watches me, trying to figure out if I'm following what he's saying. Then he removes his glasses and holds them in his left fist as if they were a weapon, and licks his lips. "From what I understand, they have quite a bit of forensic evidence, which makes our work very complicated," he continues.

"I don't know what happened there," I murmur.

"This may not be the time—" he begins.

I cut him off. "I've got nothing to hide. If I murdered him, then I deserve life in prison. I'm not the kind of guy to shirk responsibility. But I really don't know what happened that night."

"We'll have plenty of time to talk it over."

"I want to be clear right off the bat: If I murdered Crutchy Zvi, I'm willing to do prison time. No one deserves to die that way, especially not him. Got a cigarette?" I ask to keep the tears at bay.

He nods and takes a pack of cigarettes from his briefcase, pulls out two, offers me one and lights it. "I know what happened there," he says.

"At the dump?" I ask, surprised.

"Of course not. I mean in Gaza. I know what you've been through in Gaza, and they can never understand. That's why I promise you to do everything in my power to help you." His words move me deeply and give me a spark of hope.

We almost finish our cigarettes without saying anything else. Our unflinching gaze is like an embrace.

"I'm not about to claim any temporary insanity nonsense, you understand?" I finally say. "I want to figure out what happened there. I don't remember getting up from the chair, I don't remember murdering him, and I don't know how I can confess to something I can't remember."

"No one's asking you to confess," he tries to reassure me.

"The cops want me to. If they have fingerprints on the knife, his blood on my clothes, all this evidence, and they're convinced I'm the culprit, then I have to remember and confess."

"You have to calm down. Right now we aren't sure what they

have or don't have. I've never met anyone who committed murder without remembering it, you understand? I've never met anyone like that."

I feel as if he's telling me off, so I just look at him desperately.

"You have to promise me you won't confess to anything. I don't know what happened there, and right now, neither do you. You have no idea how easy it is for them to plant false memories in your head. People always think it's complicated, but I'm telling you I've seen plenty of cases where the interrogators convince a detainee of perpetrating crimes they never committed, and nothing could be easier than doing that to a defendant who can't remember the time of the crime because he was under the influence of drugs. Our memories mislead us like hallucinations. I'm intimately familiar with that," he says. I feel like, more than reassuring me, he's confessing to me. "You have to promise me that you won't do anything stupid. If you can't remember anything, then you've got nothing to confess, is that clear?"

"Only what I can remember," I say, memorizing the words like a mantra.

A few hours go by before they take me in for extended custody. On the way, in the squad car with two other detainees, each of us immersed in our own horrors, the weight of the cuffs on my wrists and ankles makes me feel as if I'll never be free again. A fly hovers through the car fearlessly. It wants to land someplace. Perhaps it's having trouble picking a spot because the entire car smells like shit.

In this very moment, just like the split second when light appears and you know dawn has broken, the entire picture becomes clear in my mind, and I want to speak to my lawyer right away. My heart is about to burst with fury and joy—fury at the Georgian, that vicious murderer, and joy because I realized there's no way I killed Crutchy Zvi. All at once, I understand everything.

The judge looks calm and friendly, like somebody's sweet grandfather, smiling and giving police officers the number of jail days they request. They present forensic evidence and that's enough, now they've got a victim and a perpetrator, but they don't have the Georgian, they don't even know about the Georgian, they know nothing about him because they don't want to know. When all the puzzle pieces fit, you don't go off looking for more pieces.

"I know who the murderer is," I whisper to my lawyer in the courtroom before being taken back down to the squad car.

He stares at me. "What does that mean?"

"It clicked for me on the way to the courthouse. I know who murdered Crutchy Zvi."

"Just like that?"

"Exactly."

His face scrunches skeptically. But I have no doubts. I know the Georgian killed Crutchy Zvi and framed me.

"Okay, I don't want you talking about it with anyone. Even if you're right, they can't hear about it before I check out your story," the lawyer says just as the police officer pulls me by the hand toward the exit. But I no longer care about being dragged, because I know. I know.

═══════

When we return to jail, they put me in a cell with a communicator. How do I know he's a communicator? Because he tries to get me to communicate with him. He does his best to be nice, playing the part of a junkie being accused of robbing a gas station. He tells me his story, and I'm supposed to tell him mine, but I remember what the lawyer told me. I say nothing.

Instead, I lie in my cot, feeling around my chest for the Uri Geller spoon, but my fingers can't find it. I don't have a spoon so I can't hold onto it and try to bend it. It's infuriating because I could have used this time here to concentrate on the spoon. What a waste of time. The communicator, who introduces himself as

Chaim, sits down on the edge of my cot. He brings his ugly face close to mine, exhaling his sour breath on me, and asks how I'm feeling, as if to intensify my need for heroin.

"I need a hit. God, my body's going crazy, my brain is on overload. Methadone just doesn't cut it, I'm telling you. It takes the edge off, but it isn't the real thing, am I right?" he asks. He makes sure to show me his arms full of holes because it's all part of his game.

I can tell he's really a junkie but I don't know him. I've never seen him on the street.

"You're not a big talker, that's fine. I also thought every person they put in the cell with me was a communicator, a snitch. Best to be cautious. But I don't care because I'm not guilty. I didn't do anything so I've got nothing to hide. What about you, my brother? I hope you've got nothing to hide, either. These people are scum. They could keep you here for an entire month. They'll interrogate you until you go crazy and then you'll be willing to sign anything they want. But I've got experience. I can help you."

"I don't need any help."

"Dude, you have no idea how much help you need," he laughs, as if derisively. "You've got no idea. You need all the help you can get. They're about to fuck you, hard. They're going to sic the entire system on you. If you ask me, you should sign a plea deal. Judges love that kind of thing these days. It saves them time and money because the system is bottlenecked. Every case they close is like a breath of fresh air. I just told my lawyer today to get me a deal. I'm willing to serve two years and then come out with a clean slate. I suggest you do the same, otherwise they'll fuck you up, and you're a whole different story. They just love winning homicide cases. It gives them prestige; it gets them on the news. That's why I say there's no other way. That's how it goes—whether or not you did it, you're guilty. Listen to Chaim—you'd better sign a deal and get it over with."

I ask him to leave me alone, but he goes on and on, as if he wants me to punch him. But I know that's what they want me to do. That way they'll have something else on me. They'll have reason to claim I'm violent. So I let him talk and at some point I can't even hear him anymore. I'm just thinking about Doris and Dog and how Doris must be pissed off at me because she has no idea what happened. She must think I just took off.

CHAPTER TWENTY-FOUR

I don't know how long I've been here. It seems like months or years. It isn't that time is crawling, it's simply gone. When they take away your freedom and your light and your fresh air, time disappears too. I get taken into interrogation, but I don't cooperate, instead repeating that they'll be getting answers from my lawyer, whose name I can't even remember. My interrogators take shifts, trying to break me. But I'm sure it was the Georgian. He promised he'd settle the score with Crutchy Zvi, and because I beat the shit out of him he decided to frame me. How hard could it have been to put the knife in my hand and cover me with blood?

I spend all day lying in my cell, thinking about my family. About my father, about Doris, and about Dog. I think about the war and the friends I had and the ones I lost. More than anything, I think about Yehoram's final seconds of life and what a great guy he used to be and how he got shot in the brain and what a lovely brain it was, with thoughts and feelings and memories, and how as soon as the bullet sliced his head open that brain became nothing but empty matter, containing nothing, not even a soul, just red and white mush, and how after that they buried him in the ground and his parents cried and his brothers and sister and his entire family stood next to us as we aimed our rifles at the sky and shot a volley in honor of Yehoram. I think about how I should have seen the military psychiatrist. I should have told him about the nightmares and how all the people we shot in Gaza screwed up my soul, and how we did it without batting an eye, and how when we made the neighborhood shake my soldiers were pleased as punch that we were hitting back after they blew up our APC and burned our friends alive, and I should have asked him how come I didn't care about all those people. Then he would have asked me to tell him everything from the beginning, because that's how they operate, those psychiatrists. They want you to talk and listen to yourself, and when you hear the words spoken in your own voice, you understand them a little differently. He probably would have given me meds, too—these days everybody takes meds in order to be able to sleep and not be depressed and anxious. But I'd be most interested in asking him why none of this bothered me until Yuval shot that poor dog in the head. After they find the Georgian, that's exactly what I'm going to do. I'll go to the military psychiatrist and tell him about everything that happened in Shejaiya.

Trying not to think too much about Gaza, I look for something I could try bending with my mind. Even though they took away my Geller spoon, I could try something else. There aren't a lot of things in my cell, but eventually I manage to break one of the springs in the cot above mine, and since then I've been trying to bend it with the power of my mind.

I don't think the most important part about the Uri Geller bit was the spoon. Metal is metal, whether it's a spoon or a bedspring. I don't talk to the metal or rub it. I just focus all of my attention on it, aiming my thoughts like a laser beam, feeling them warming the metal. I have a good feeling about it this time. I'm sure that in a few days I'll find a way to bend the spring, and then my life will change.

Strange, but I've been eating much better than I have for the past year. This is no hotel suite, but compared to the smelly, moldy dump where I ate poorly, I feel a palpable difference. Chaim the Communicator won't stop complaining about the food, which tells me he must not be a full-blown junkie who lives on the street. I'm convinced every time he gets called out for so-called questioning he actually goes outside and wolfs down a bunch of shawarma.

The only thing missing for me is heroin. They give me methadone, which isn't exactly the same, but it pulls me off the jonesing ledge.

They take me into questioning, seat me in Katzav's office. I already know this office so well that I'm starting to feel kind of comfortable here, and I can't help but think how my father would lose his shit if he saw me sitting spread-legged in an interrogation room like a battle-scarred criminal.

"Good morning," Katzav says, smiling. "I've got a surprise for you, Geller."

I lower my eyes.

"Someone's here to visit you," he says smugly.

As soon as the door behind me opens, I know who's there to see me. Maybe it's because of the scent of his cologne that I can tell it's Avihai, my commander. At first I feel his heavy hand on my shoulder, his fingers squeezing. And his squeeze contains friendship and longing and anger. I can sense lots of things from Avihai's squeeze.

Katzav gets up and shakes Avihai's hand. I don't turn around yet. I catch their handshake from the corner of my eye. Katzav's hand looks minuscule inside of Avihai's enormous paw. He was always big and muscular. Maybe that's why we all followed him blindly. A man of Avihai's dimensions gives the impression that everything is small potatoes.

Now I feel him standing over me. Katzav leaves the room, and Avihai looks right at me. I don't dare raise my eyes to meet his. I can smell his uniform, smell his rifle and tourniquet and gun oil and cologne, all of these smells that I haven't smelled in so long, not since my last stint of reserve duty. These aromas of men, of combatants, of brothers in arms.

"Barak," Avihai says.

I don't respond. I don't know who Barak is. He hasn't been in my body for months. "They call me Geller now," I say.

He nods as he sits down in Katzav's chair. But he's so much more powerful than Katzav. He takes up almost the entire office. He must have had to deposit his rifle before they let him in. I don't remember ever seeing him without it. "You'll always be Barak to me," he says.

We sit for a while, staring at each other, and I think about how we used to sit together, all the officers, in pre-drill meetings or in operation briefings. But back then, we looked at each other differently.

"There's just one thing I don't get," he says, breaking the silence. His voice sounds just like back then, and it makes me feel so small, because I guess no matter how many years go by, one always idolizes their commanders. "How did you get this far gone without talking to me? Without talking to anyone from the unit?"

"Things just happened," I find myself muttering.

"Just happened my ass. Don't you remember how we all showed up for Pinto when he needed help? How we collected money for Gili's daughter? Man, I've been looking for you for months, and all your mother can say is that she doesn't know what's going on with you. She must have been too embarrassed to tell me."

"Leave my mother out of this, Avihai. She doesn't deserve this after what she's been through with my father."

"Yes, the stroke. I know about that."

As I nod, he asks, "So what happened? Would you tell me what happened?"

"Everything came back to haunt me. Shejaiya and all our people that were killed there and all the people we killed, and Yehoram. They all came back and drove me crazy." I give it to him straight, no shame.

Avihai's face shows pity, then anger. He shifts between emotions so quickly that it confuses me. "You listen to me now. I'm going to help you. Your team is going to help you. The unit will do whatever is necessary. We're brothers, and brothers help each other out," he says.

I think about how my brother once wanted to help me, which only pissed me off. But for some reason, I'm not angry now. I look at him and am filled with profound sorrow, and all of a sudden I tell him about Dog. Out of everything that happened, Dog, and how I can't get the image of Yuval shooting Dog out of my head.

Avihai says nothing at first. His face is as hard as rock. I see his hand twitching, as if searching for his rifle. He clears his throat and the shadow of a smile flashes across his face, an almost invisible tic that vanishes instantly, replaced with tiny gestures of discomfort. "How do you manage here?" he asks.

I can't answer him. He's hiding something from me. He's trying to change the subject and it makes my blood boil. "You're keeping something from me," I mutter.

By the way he looks at me, I can tell it's true. Now his eyes are evading, but he says, "It's not important." Three words that hit me like fists.

"Don't decide for me what's important and what isn't, okay? I was there, just like you. I saw everybody die. I carried Yehoram in my arms and took a bullet to the thigh and a bullet to the shoulder," I shout.

"You're a hero, my brother," Avihai says.

"Don't fuck with me, Avihai, and don't belittle me!"

"What do you want to hear, man? What the hell do you want to hear?" Now it's his turn to yell at me. "We were all in that shit. What do you want me to tell you? That we were sons of bitches? We weren't. It's war, and things happen in war, people get killed in war, including innocents, including civilians. In war people lose friends and blow up and get burned alive in APCs. So I don't know what you want to hear."

"I want you to tell me the truth, Avihai. What is it? What are you hiding?" I ask, wiping the spittle from my lips with my sleeve.

Avihai looks at me, his eyes piercing, his left hand cupping his right fist. "Yuval didn't shoot the dog."

His words fall to the floor, shattering into a million pieces. The room is full of them. No matter where I step, I'll get hurt. No matter where I place my hand, I'll get cut.

"You were the biggest son of a bitch of all, is that what you want to hear? You were tough shit. You even shot those who didn't need to be shot. You were willing to pay any price to protect your soldiers, and you killed anyone who got in your way. You're the one who shot that poor dog in the head."

After he finishes talking, I hear nothing but silence. It's as if a bomb just went off in the room and the shockwave has rendered me temporarily deaf. I try to recall it, but I can't. All the images that flash through my head, from wartime, from Gaza, are confused. I can't see myself, only Yuval shooting Dog in the head.

"You're lying," I tell Avihai. But his face isn't lying. His lip isn't twitching; his eyes are determined and honest. "I remember Yuval killing Dog. I remember him cocking his Glock against his belt and shooting poor Dog in the head. I was there, Avihai, I remember."

"I'm sorry, Barak, but you're wrong."

I don't hear the door opening, but all of a sudden, Katzav is standing beside me, undoing the cuffs around my wrists and ankles. "You're free to go," he says. "They found the murderer's clothes in a construction container not far from your place. We arrested a suspect known as the Georgian. He already confessed and told us everything that happened," he says, slapping my back as if he wasn't trying to ruin my life until just a minute ago.

But I don't want to leave. I want to go back to my cell. I deserve to go back to that cell.

"Someone named Doris is waiting for you outside," Katzav adds.

Avihai gets up and gives me a tight, tough commander hug. But I feel nothing. I see nothing. Nothing but Dog's face.

AUTHOR'S NOTE

I enlisted in the IDF in November 1990, joining an elite unit. I endured grueling training and operated in hostile territory. During my service, I encountered complex situations and witnessed sights that the human soul struggles to endure. I was a sensitive, dreamy teenager, and I had no way of knowing that these horrors would seep through my uniform, past the oil of my rifle, through the cracks in my calloused skin, and reach straight to my heart.

I experienced life-threatening situations. I saw lifeless bodies. Outwardly, I was filled with testosterone, ego, and masculinity, but inside, my soul was in turmoil, desperately trying to protect itself in any way possible. After I completed my military service, I enrolled in psychology studies. While juggling school and work, I began using drugs and alcohol daily. My life unfolded in a haze of intoxication. I met and fell in love with Elinor, we had our first-born son, and all the while, I continued to escape reality through addictive substances. Some nights, I would wake up in terror from nightmares. Some nights, I would hit Elinor in my sleep.

Elinor pleaded with me to seek treatment. She knew I was suffering from combat trauma, but my masculine ego continued to govern me. I could not admit that my soul had been wounded.

I began writing *Dog* in the winter of 2018, after I had already replaced drugs and alcohol with psychiatric medication—antidepressants and anti-anxiety pills—but I was still in complete denial that my psyche had been injured during my combat service. I believed my anxiety and panic attacks were a consequence of substance abuse.

Years after I had written the first draft of *Dog*, during the COVID-19 pandemic, my former unit decided to organize a reunion. It was an emotional gathering after years of separation. We caught up, relived old memories, and shared stories from our service. I returned home, and the next day, I woke up feeling physically ill—it was, perhaps, a signal that my soul could no longer bear the heavy burden. In the days that followed, waves of anxiety and panic crashed over me. Days stretched into weeks and months of relentless terror.

For the first time, I understood that I was suffering from PTSD. That I needed treatment. That I needed official recognition from the military for my injury.

Today, I realize that the writer within me knew I was a combat trauma survivor long before I did. The writer in me wrote *Dog* because I could not admit it myself. I thought that being a combat trauma survivor was a weakness, a wound to my ego and masculinity.

Now, I know that those who suffer from combat trauma are warriors who have been wounded in their souls, just as others have lost a limb. It is not their fault, and they should not feel shame.

ACKNOWLEDGMENTS

Books, like stray dogs, don't find their way into the world alone. They need patience, care, and the kindness of those who see their worth.

First and foremost, to my family—your love is the home I return to, the steady ground beneath my feet. Your unwavering belief in me has been my anchor in the chaos of creation, and without you, *Dog* would have remained just a whisper in my mind.

To **Yardenne Greenspan**, who took my words and carried them across borders and languages, preserving their soul in every line—your translation is a bridge, and I am forever grateful for your craftsmanship.

To **Michael Pye**, Advisory Board Member of Soncata Press— who recognized *Dog*'s spirit from the first page. Your keen eye and decades of publishing wisdom helped shape it into the book it was meant to be. I am grateful beyond words.

To **Howard Grossman**, who gave *Dog* its face. A book cover isn't just an image—it's a promise, an invitation. Your design captured the spirit of this story in a single moment, and for that, I am thankful.

To **Liza Darnton**, whose sharp editorial instincts helped carve this novel into its truest form. Your insight and guidance made *Dog* stronger, and I am fortunate to have had your voice in this process.

To **Rita Lewis** and **Karin Wiberg** of Clear Sight Books—thank you for helping us navigate *Dog* through the final stretch.

To **Ann Marie Sabath**—a publisher like you is a rare gift. Your belief in this book, your vision, and your tireless efforts have made *Dog* more than just a novel—it is now something that can be shared, felt, and lived. I am deeply grateful for your trust and support.

And to **you, the reader**—thank you for stepping into this story, for carrying it with you, for allowing these pages to become part of your world. Every book is incomplete without the eyes that read it, the hearts that feel it. You bring *Dog* to life in ways I could never have imagined.

With gratitude,

Ishi Ron

BOOK CLUB STUDY GUIDE

In *Dog*, Yishay Ishi Ron delivers a haunting and deeply human exploration of trauma, addiction, and redemption. The novel follows Geller, a former elite soldier suffering from severe PTSD, as he navigates the fringes of society, clinging to heroin and memories that refuse to release him. A dog, a woman named Doris, and a city that both shelters and devours him all intertwine in his battle for survival. With sharp prose and devastating honesty, *Dog* is a novel that lingers in the mind long after the final page.

But *Dog* is more than Geller's story. It is the story of so many soldiers who return from war with wounds no one can see. It is the story of the burdens they carry, the streets they wander, the hope they chase—and the pain they struggle to understand.

Discussion Questions

1. The Role of the Dog – What does Dog represent in Geller's life? How does their bond serve as an emotional anchor for him? Were you surprised by the revelation of who actually killed Dog?

2. Memory and Perception – Throughout the novel, Geller's grasp on reality is unstable. How does the novel portray the ways trauma distorts memory? Did you trust Geller as a narrator? Why or why not?

3. The Betrayal of Memory – The moment Geller learns the truth about Dog's death is a pivotal turning point. How does this revelation affect the way we understand his entire journey? What does it say about trauma's ability to warp reality?

4. The Impact of War – The novel delves deeply into the long-term effects of war. How does *Dog* portray PTSD differently from other war novels you've read? What do you think the book suggests about the responsibility of a society toward its veterans?

5. Masculinity and Vulnerability – Geller resists seeking help, believing it to be a sign of weakness. How does *Dog* challenge traditional notions of masculinity, especially in the context of soldiers and war?

6. Survivor's Guilt – Geller repeatedly questions why he survived when so many of his comrades didn't. How does survivor's guilt manifest in his actions and choices? Do you think he ever truly wants to live, or is he simply avoiding death?

7. Doris as a Figure of Redemption – Doris offers Geller shelter, comfort, and a semblance of normalcy. What role does she play in his journey? Do you think she genuinely helps him, or does she represent a kind of temporary escape?

8. **The Spoon as a Symbol** – Geller clings to the Uri Geller spoon as a kind of talisman. What do you think it represents for him? How does it relate to his longing for control and belief in miracles?

9. **The Murder of Crutchy Zvi** – Geller is accused of murder but has no memory of it. How does this uncertainty affect your perception of him? Did you believe in his innocence from the beginning?

10. **Addiction and Survival** – The novel does not shy away from the realities of addiction. How does *Dog* challenge common narratives about drug use and homelessness? Did it shift your perspective on addiction?

11. **The Ending and Geller's Revelation** – The final revelation about Dog's death is devastating. How does this shift your understanding of Geller's guilt and self-perception? Does this moment redefine the entire novel for you?

12. **Justice and Redemption** – Now that the Georgian has been arrested, what do you think lies ahead for Geller? Do you believe he can heal, or is he too deeply scarred?

13. **Title Significance** – Why do you think the novel is titled *Dog*? How does the title take on different meanings throughout the book?

Frequently Asked Questions

1. Is *Dog* based on a true story?
While *Dog* is a work of fiction, it is deeply personal and inspired by my own experiences with PTSD, addiction, and trauma. Many elements of the novel are drawn from reality, though the story itself is not autobiographical.

2. Why did you choose to tell the story through Geller's perspective?
Geller's fractured, unreliable perception mirrors the way trauma and addiction distort reality. His perspective forces the reader to experience his confusion and suffering firsthand.

3. Why is the revelation about Dog's death so important?
The moment Geller realizes he was the one who killed Dog is the culmination of everything the novel explores—memory, guilt, trauma, and self-destruction. It is the ultimate betrayal of his own mind.

4. What message do you hope readers take from *Dog*?
That trauma is real, that it can destroy lives, and that those who suffer from it deserve compassion, not judgment.

5. Why does the novel focus so much on addiction?
Because addiction is often a symptom of a deeper wound. *Dog* explores addiction not as a moral failing, but as a desperate attempt to numb unbearable pain.

6. What is the significance of the Uri Geller spoon?
It represents control, hope, and the longing to reverse the irreversible—to bend fate itself.

7. How does *Dog* challenge the traditional war novel?
It does not glorify war or focus on the battlefield, but rather on the unseen wounds soldiers carry home.

8. How do you see Doris's role in Geller's story?
She represents the possibility of human connection, but also the limits of what another person can do to save someone who does not want to be saved.

9. Will there be a sequel?
No, *Dog* is a standalone novel.

PREVIEW OF

The Girl Who Rode the White Lion

by Yishay Ishi Ron

Thank you for reading *Dog*. I hope you enjoyed it. As a special treat, here's a sneak-peak of my next book, *The Girl Who Rode the White Lion*.

The story takes place in two timelines. The first begins in the city of Darmstadt, Germany, on November 9, 1938, during Kristall-nacht, and follows the plight of the young girl Sarah Frank and her escape from the SS officer, Hauptsturmführer Hubert Zimmer. She finds refuge in the marvelous circus of Adolf Frey. Adolf, the circus owner and famous lion trainer, is married to Louise, a French woman and elephant trainer, who hides her Jewish identity. The circus has already committed to performances in German cities, but Adolf's plans are disrupted when the SS officer, search-ing for Sarah, shows no intention of giving up.

The second timeline of the book takes place in New York City on January 6, 1957, when Mark Spencer, a veterinarian at the Central Park Zoo, performs a post-mortem examination on a rare white lion named Christmas, and discovers an SS ring made of silver inside its stomach.

How did the SS ring end up in the lion's belly? Mark Spencer becomes embroiled in a mystery that takes him to Florida, France, Israel, and back to New York. The two timelines eventually con-verge as the mystery is solved.

Turn the page to begin reading!

CHAPTER ONE

Darmstadt, Germany
November 9th, 1938

Before he knew it, the hour grew late, and Hauptsturmführer Hubert Zimmer's mind was exhausted from pondering. Hours of anticipation roiled through his mind, racking his nerves with alertness and expectation of what the night had devised for him. Distractedly, he played with his silver skull ring the way people mindlessly bite their fingernails or crack their knuckles. He'd received the ring earlier that year, at his rank promotion ceremony— a sign of respect from Reichsführer Heinrich Himmler himself. To Hubert Zimmer, it was like a wedding ring.

The Hauptsturmführer's office was gray and depressing, a reflection of his own hackneyed, unglamorous visage. The walls were naked of any decoration and the furniture was sparse and industrial. In the corner was a radiator, and above it a small window sealed with milky whitewash. As far as the Hauptsturmführer could recall, it had never been opened. The air was therefore heavy and thick, laden with the smoke of Overstolz cigarettes, the butts of which were overflowing from a heavy glass ashtray with notched sides.

In his black uniform, he sat in the cushy interrogator's chair at a heavy desk. Upon it, a reading lamp springing from a long and narrow stork leg overlooked an ink well, the department's stamp, a block of paper, and a fountain pen, all arranged with the meticulousness of a surgeon. Across from him were two hard, simple, uncomfortable seats—appropriate for suspects undergoing interrogations.

To his left was a chest of drawers full of news articles that never stopped coming, filed in folders containing details and extensive descriptions of civilians who've had the distinct misfortune of drawing the attention of the SS. The public assumed that the SS was everywhere; that hundreds of thousands of agents were walking among them, digging into their actions, eavesdropping on their conversations, listening to their whispered secrets, and rummaging through their personal belongings. But in truth, most investigations against civilians were initiated by reports received from informants. Within a short amount of time, with the help of Reichsführer Heinrich Himmler, an entire nation had been transformed into a squad of secret agents snitching on each other.

Hubert opened the desk drawer and pulled out a metal flask wrapped in a firm suit of aged, cracked leather. After a generous swig of whiskey, he felt a burning in his esophagus. A warm euphoria spread through his head, and he wiped his lips on the sleeve of the jacket before rising, leaning his hands against the desk, and drawing a deep breath.

This was a special day for him; a landmark as real as the pin on his lapel. He pushed the chair back and paced the room, dragging his left leg—a memento from his childhood Osteomyelitis. Over the years, he'd learned to compensate for the limp by balancing out his position, which involved strutting like a rooster and led his schoolmates to tease him mercilessly.

He sat back down, took hold of the armrests, and exhaled heavily, trying to push the distress out of his body. Children are among the most horrific kind of monsters. His prominent limp provided every eager little rascal with all the ammunition they needed. From time to time, during recess, the schoolyard seemed to become a chicken coop, featuring children mimicking silly walks through bursts of crowing laughter and nasty comments. He was the victim of aspiring young poets who added music to their rhyming limericks about the limping rooster.

His appearance was also cause for shame: a prominent nose, black hair, and a wiry frame—a stereotypically Jewish look. His eyes were asymmetrical and his nose and mouth were too close together, making him look like a pointy bird. And those scoundrels missed nothing. They called him *jüdischer vogel*—Jewish Bird, a nickname that stayed with him for years, causing him no shortage of agony. As an adult, he consoled himself with the knowledge that his limp resembled that of Herr Goebbels and that his hair was as black as the führer's, but he never dared point that out to his colleagues. A comment like that could cost him his job, or worse.

When he joined the Nazi Party, he did his best to prove his allegiance. He swore to defend the führer and the homeland. Many wanted to take away what the führer had earned with sweat, and Hubert Zimmer planned to do everything in his power in order to protect the country from the Jewish dogs and the dirty communists.

Time ticked by languidly. It was the habit of anticipation to slow down the clock. He pulled up his sleeve and glanced at his watch. Horboch and Hempel would be back any minute with reports from the field, and he would lead a squadron of young recruits and embark on a quest for arrests. He was bubbling with excitement like a boiling cauldron. The aroma of violence was palpable, just like the words that left Herr Goebbels's mouth and crashed like boulders over the heads of the Jews. It was time for the enemies of the state to pay for their crimes. Those Israelites who brought on the loss of the Great War, who sat in their dim offices on heaps on money stolen from laborers that worked themselves down to the bone and survived on scraps. Tonight it would begin: the orders instructed that every Jewish man, aged sixty or younger should be detained and sent off to the Buchenwald

Concentration Camp. Only once they got rid of all the Jews and Germany was finally clean could the Third Reich truly be built.

Frau Kejtel knocked on his door, shaking away his reveries. "Hauptsturmführer, the lists have arrived," she said as she walked in, laying a stack of papers on his desk.

He thanked her politely, his nostrils flaring to inhale the intoxicating bergamot fragrance of her body. He tried to maintain a calm demeanor, his thumb almost uncontrollably fluttering over the silver ring. When she leaned closer, his bespectacled eyes fixed on the neckline of her blouse, where her flesh curved on its way up to the hills of her enormous breasts. Then he got a hold of himself, took a deep, quiet breath, and allowed the citrus aroma to flow through his arteries and fill him with intense desire. What he wouldn't give to bed this perfect woman. His tongue dampened his thin lips. A true Aryan with a strong, sturdy Nordic build, long and smooth yolk-toned hair, fair skin, and tall stature. A beauty whose baby blue eyes were veiled with eroticism. He was only able to love her in fantasies of fornication, dreaming of her with insatiable lust.

He had no chance of landing such a woman anywhere apart from at Frau Greta Wieler's brothel. He knew that some officers regularly patronized her establishment, but he was too shy and awkward to show his face at such a place. He'd always avoided the company of other humans. First as a child, then as a young man, he was disgusted by the shape of his body and the reflection of his face in the mirror. He was skinny and pale and terrified, and felt he would likely grow up to become a man that women were not attracted to. His isolation forced him to endure many hours of boredom. But as a police officer, his shortcoming became an advantage, and the long hours he spent at the job bought him the respect of his commanders, who recognized his industriousness and promoted him swiftly.

He lived with his elderly parents, a couple of sickly retirees, in a cramped apartment the smell of which was enough to fill him with glum misery—a smell that clung to the walls and the furniture and could not be eliminated even through a deep cleaning. Cabbage, sausages, potatoes, concentrated sweat, cigarette smoke, and alcohol—an astringent combination of sour rot.

His father used to slap him, punch him, and whip him with a belt. From time to time, just for laughs, he would offer him a swift kick in the ass, then double up with laughter as if he'd just heard a hilarious joke. He was also the first person to ever mock Hubert's limp, teaching him what shame was by appearing mortified with his very existence. The father was a crude, bitter, critical man, not easily satisfied; a hard-working heavy drinker.

His mother, who often suffered from the man's violence, was a more amiable creature, but devoid of all talents and capabilities. She was but a ghost, unable to defend her son or lift his spirits. Their home was never a pleasant place to be—neither during his childhood, nor now.

Hubert Zimmer watched Frau Kejtel's seductive rear-end as she walked away. Only when the door closed did he look down at the list. He dampened his finger against his tongue and flipped through the pages, quickly scanning the last names until he reached the letter F. His heart fluttered with anticipation similar to the kind one feels before reuniting with a family member returning from a prolonged absence. His fingers marked an invisible line under each line of names and addresses pristinely composed in a typewriter with black ink: *Furst, Fleischman, Fliesing,* and finally *Frank*— 7 Schlossgarten Street, across from the royal gardens.

He folded the papers and stuffed them into his jacket pocket. He'd known Jozef Frank since they were children. They grew up together and would spend every afternoon playing in the thicket behind school. They stood by each other when the neighborhood children picked on them. Hubert was often victimized due to Jozef's Judaism, and Jozef suffered for Hubert's limp.

Hubert's parents were not pleased by their friendship. They'd never been too fond of Jews. But the Frank family embraced him.

That was the way of the Jews. They were as sly as snakes, and always had a secret motive for bonding with Aryan Germans.

Years later, when the Great War broke, they parted ways. Jozef Frank was recruited to the Imperial Armed Forces while Hubert stayed on at the arms factory, which needed all the help it could get from the women, the elderly, and disabled Hubert Zimmer.

Jozef Frank returned at the end of the war, decorated with medals and officer ranks, and was accepted into the Munich School of Medicine. Just like back in their schooldays, he excelled at his studies. They exchanged letters for a while. In fact, Jozef Frank was the one who recommended that Hubert enlist in the police force, and while Hubert viewed this as an insult, he knew he was unfit for higher learning, and took his friend's advice.

For several years, Jozef was Hubert's doctor. But when the Nazis rose to power, and especially after the Nuremberg Laws were enacted, it was no longer appropriate for a Gestapo officer to be treated by a Jewish doctor. In an act of solidarity, Hubert abandoned his friend and switched to Dr. Friek Rudolf, a German doctor. An Aryan.

Over the years, the inferiority he felt in the presence of Jozef Frank intensified. Here was a successful Jew from a wealthy family, keen of mind and handsome. Though they had a long mutual history, the man caused him more pain than good.

Hubert's hatred for Jews grew fiercer due to the influence of Julius Streicher's newspaper *Der Stürmer*, the führer and Herr Goebbels's eloquent speeches, and the party's dramatic propaganda films. He recalled the times he'd visited the doctor's home—a large estate with a wonderful garden and two tall trees shading the entrance. A German servant would escort him to the waiting room, or, if he was lucky it was the doctor's beautiful wife—the exquisite Ruth Frank—who opened the door.

He hated her even more than he hated his friend, because her beauty was matched only by the fact that she belonged to Jozef Frank. She had a childlike face, full black hair, and a cherry mouth, and she smelled of the sweet but fresh perfume of female skin, as warm and smooth as milk. She was certainly the most coveted prize a man could earn, and that man was Jozef Frank.

Hubert would flip through a magazine until the doctor became available, and had no doubt that his friend kept him waiting longer than necessary, even when he wasn't with another patient, simply in order to emphasize the class divide between them. This sensation didn't leave him even when Jozef Frank finally greeted him with a friendly smile and a warm handshake, never forgetting to ask his wife to serve Hubert a cup of tea and a piece of cake.

Sometimes, when she knew her husband would be delayed, Ruth invited Hubert into the kitchen, where they would have a drink and a chat. Hubert would imagine himself married to the Jew's wife, prattling with her about their children while she cooked the Jewish dishes that, he had to admit, smelled delicious.

How he wished now that he could see his friend's face. An unforgettable sight! But the Hauptsturmführer's excitement was diluted by fear and befuddlement. He felt like a man about to sentence his own father.

ABOUT THE AUTHOR

YISHAY ISHI RON served in an elite IDF combat unit and is a survivor of PTSD. He has channeled his experiences into his writing, with his U.S. debut novel, *Dog*, offering a raw portrayal of a soldier grappling with trauma and addiction. The novel, originally written in Hebrew, was longlisted for the Sapir Prize, one of Israel's most prestigious literary awards. His next novel, *The Girl Who Rode the White Lion*, will be released in 2026. Yishay Ishi Ron is married and lives near Tel Aviv with his wife and three children.

Yishay Ishi Ron occasionally steps out from behind the page—usually to post something thoughtful, strange, or unexpectedly tender. You can find him on Instagram, where he shares behind-the-scenes glimpses, reflections on trauma and language, and proof that even writers sometimes leave the house. He also wanders through X (formerly Twitter) and Facebook when the mood strikes, especially if there's a good story waiting.

Connect with Yishay on:

- Instagram: @yishayishiron
- X (formerly Twitter): @IshiRon1
- Facebook: Yishay.Ron.1

Stay updated about upcoming events by visiting the author's website at www.yishayishiron.com.

Contact the author at yishayishiron@gmail.com.

ABOUT THE TRANSLATOR

Yardenne Greenspan is a writer and Hebrew translator born in Tel Aviv. Her work has been featured in *Tablet, Jewish Book Council, Literary Hub, Haaretz, Words Without Borders*, and as a regular column in *Ploughshares*. Her translations have been published by Restless Books, St. Martin's Press, Akashic, New Vessel Press, Amazon Crossing, and Farrar, Straus & Giroux. Her translation of *The Memory Monster* by Yishai Sarid was a 2020 *New York Times* Notable Book, and her translations have repeatedly been included in World Literature Today's Notable Translations lists. Greenspan has taught creative writing and translation workshops at Columbia University and at a VA hospital. Yardenne has an MFA from Columbia University and lives in New York City.

Connect with Yardenne on:
- Instagram: @yardennegreenspan
- X (formerly Twitter): @Yardenne
- Facebook: Yardenne Greenspan

9 798999 264524